Trevor Holman was born in England, and was brought up and educated in South London, where he worked for many years as a professional musician before moving to Norfolk, also in the UK. For most of that time, Trevor's career was centred around the music world and the advertising industry, all the while serving in court as a magistrate.

In 2003, Trevor and his wife Frances moved to the Algarve, where he began a fruitful collaboration with a local lyricist. The two of them have written in excess of one hundred songs, as well as four complete stage musicals about characters as diverse as Sir Winston Churchill, Admiral Lord Horatio Nelson and Napoleon Bonaparte, Al Capone and the Apostle Paul. Trevor is now concentrating full time on his writing career, and is currently working on this series of 'Algarve Crime Thrillers', of which 'The Mijas Murderer' is the first. Trevor and his wife still live in the Algarve.

Dedication

Dedicated to Valerie Corney
My best friend in the Algarve

Trevor Holman

THE MIJAS MURDERER

AUSTIN MACAULEY PUBLISHERS™
London • Cambridge • New York • Sharjah

Ordering Information:
Quantity sales: special discounts are available on quantity purchases by corporations, associations, and others. For details, contact the publisher at the address below.

Holman Trevor.
The Mijas Murderer

ISBN 9781947353787 (Paperback)
ISBN 9781947353800 (Hardback)
ISBN 9781947353794 (E-Book

The main category of the book Modern & contemporary fiction (post c 1945) (FA), Other category Crime & mystery (FF) Another subject category Thriller / suspense (FH)

www.austinmacauley.com/us

First Published (2018)
Austin Macauley Publishers ™ LLC
40 Wall Street, 28th Floor
New York, NY 10005
USA

mail-usa@austinmacauley.com
+1 (646) 5125767

Acknowledgement

I would like to acknowledge the support of my wonderful wife Frances, who always encourages me in whatever crazy ideas and schemes I come up with, including the writing of this book.

Characters in the Book

Algarve, Portugal :

Michael Turner	Me. Murder Mystery Writer
Dr Sam Clark	Private Doctor
Jan Cochrane	Sam's Receptionist
Malcolm Tisbury	Diamond Dealer
Inspector Paulo Cabrita	Portuguese GNR Officer

Spain :

Derek Simpson	Diamond Thief
Sandra Simpson	Derek Simpson's Wife
Freddie Drayton	Derek Simpson's Enforcer
Jimmy Priestly	Derek Simpson's Chauffer
Alex Donovan	Derek Simpson's Muscle
Dominic St Clair	Derek Simpson's Lawyer
General Carlos Bautista	Regional Head of Guardia Civil

London:

Superintendent Stephen Colshaw	Metropolitan Police
Detective Inspector Paul Naismith	Metropolitan Police
Detective Sergeant Richard Thorpe	Metropolitan Police
Jeremy Green	Malcolm Tisbury's Shop Manager
Caroline Chambers	Malcolm Tisbury's God Daughter

South Africa :

Markus Dressler	De Beers Chairman
Marius Van der Byl	De Beers New Business Director
Francois Viljoen	De Beers Courier Manager
Pieter Van Straaten	De Beers Courier
Jan Joubert	De Beers Courier
Captain Kurt Meisner	Interpol Senior Liaison Officer
Martin Smith	Interpol Burglar

Amsterdam, Netherlands:

Brigadier Helena Van Houten	Interpol Liaison Officer
Hannes de Jaeger	Diamond Cutter & Polisher

Bahamas :

Naomi Gardiner	Thaxted's Office Manager
Casandra Dufreine	Naomi Gardiner's PA

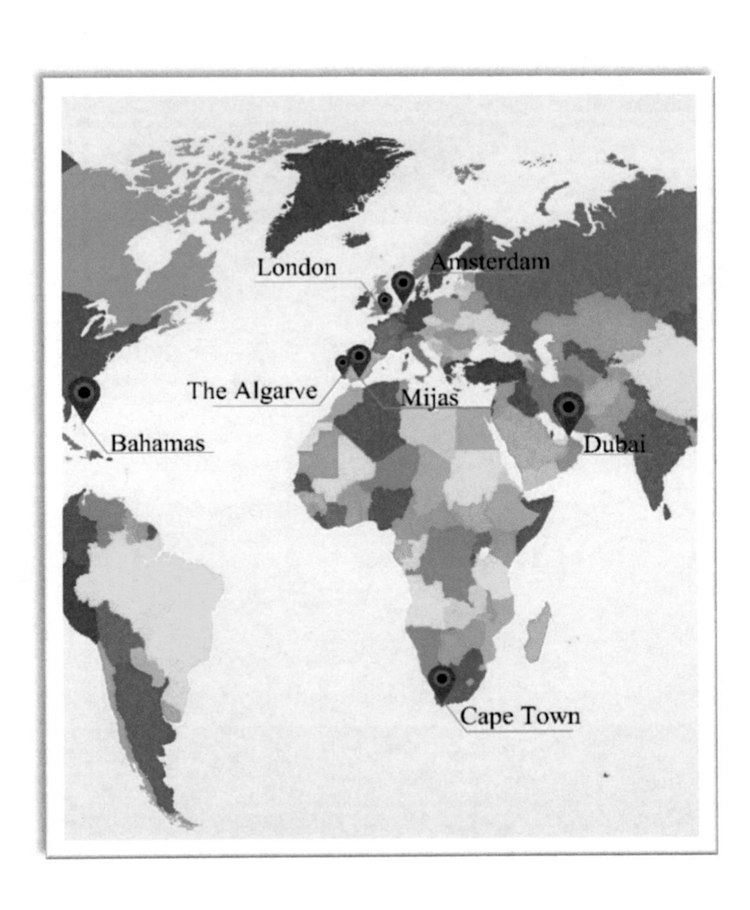
London
Amsterdam
The Algarve
Mijas
Bahamas
Dubai
Cape Town

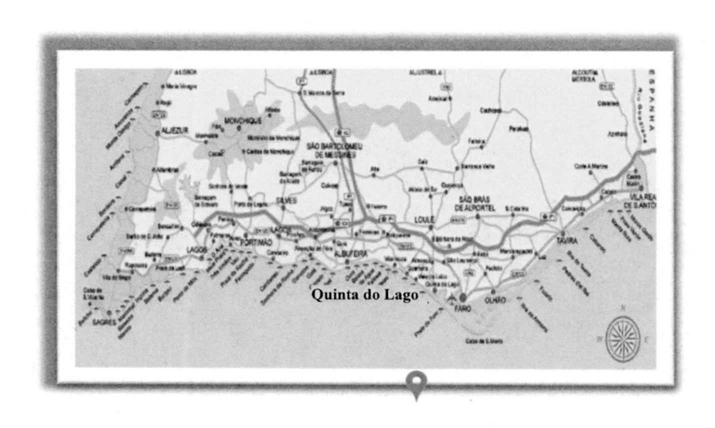
ALJEZUR
MONCHIQUE
SÃO BARTOLOMEU
DE MESSINES
SILVES
LOULÉ
SÃO BRÁS
DE ALPORTEL
LAGOS
PORTIMÃO
ALBUFEIRA
TAVIRA
Quinta do Lago
FARO
OLHÃO
SAGRES
ESPANHA

Ronda
Yunquera
Parque Natural
Sierra de
las Nieves
Tolox
Estacion
de Cartama
Cártama
A-7
Málaga
Coín
Alhaurín
el Grande
Alhaurín
de la Torre
MA-20
Torremolinos
Benalmádena
Júzcar
Mijas
Istán
Jubrique
Ojén
Fuengirola
Benahavís
Marbella
AP-7
A-7
La Cala
de Mijas
San Pedro
de Alcántara
Estepona
San Luis de
Sabinillas
AP-7
COSTA DE SOL

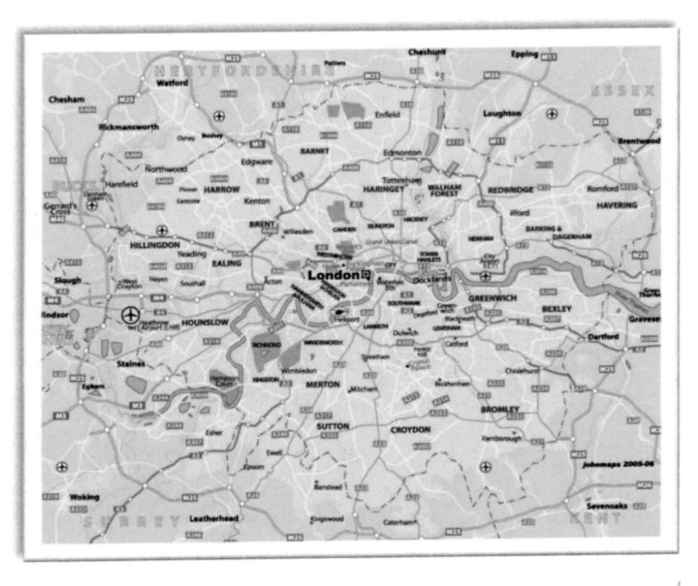
HERTFORDSHIRE
ESSEX
SURREY
KENT
Cheshunt
Epping
Watford
Chesham
Rickmansworth
Enfield
Loughton
BARNET
Edmonton
Brentwood
Northwood
Edgware
Harefield
HARROW
Kenton
HARINGEY
WALHAM FOREST
REDBRIDGE
Romford
HAVERING
BRENT
Ilford
HILLINGDON
Yeading
EALING
London
Slough
Southall
Acton
Docklands
GREENWICH
BEXLEY
HOUNSLOW
Heliport
Gravesend
Dartford
Staines
Wimbledon
MERTON
Mitcham
BROMLEY
SUTTON
CROYDON
Esher
Epsom
Farnborough
johomaps 2005-06
Woking
Leatherhead
Sevenoaks

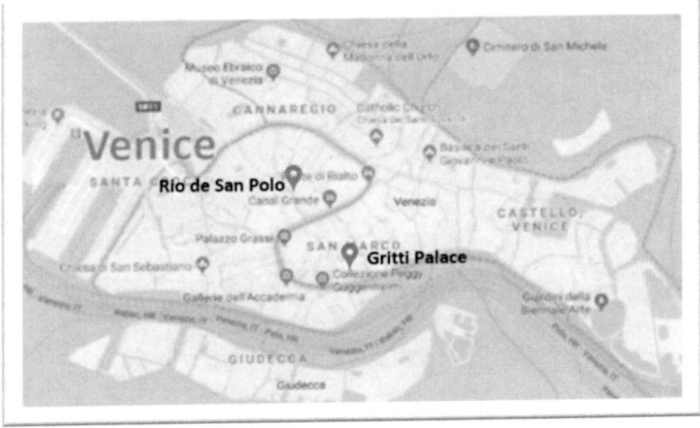
Venice
CANNAREGIO
Rio de San Polo
Canal Grande
Venezia
CASTELLO, VENICE
Palazzo Grassi
Gritti Palace
Chiesa di San Sebastiano
Gallerie dell'Accademia
GIUDECCA
Giudecca
Cimitero di San Michele
Museo Ebraico di Venezia

Oostzaan
Lands-
meer
Watergang
A10
Zunder-
dorp
Noord
Amsterdam
Centrum
West
Nieuw-
West
Oost
A10
Zuid
Duiven-
drecht
Diemen
Zuidoost
Amsterdam

Chapter One

Hi. My name is Michael Turner. I'm thirty-eight years old and a reasonably successful murder-mystery and travel writer.

I first thought I'd try my hand at writing when I was twenty-three years old. I was working in advertising sales for a publisher that had a string of technical magazines, but I wanted to try something a bit different. My first effort was a story about a bunch of London criminals who broke into a series of underground bank vaults in the middle of the night. I knew London reasonably well as it happened to be where I lived at the time, and once I'd finished writing the book, I emailed copies to several publishers, including the publisher of my favourite writer—Frederick Forsyth. I'd just finished reading his book "The Fist of God", a lengthy novel about the Gulf war, and I just loved the way he wrote his stories. Lots of detailed research and a great mixture of fact and fiction to such an extent that you as the reader hadn't a clue what was fact and what was fiction. I decided I'd try to follow suit and base my writing style on that of my literary hero.

Unfortunately for me, it soon became pretty obvious that I was no Frederick Forsyth, and my writing was not up to scratch. But one of the many publishers I'd sent my book to told me in an email reply that they might be interested if I took the time to re-write a few sections of the book. They were the only publishers that didn't say a flat no to my efforts, so I jumped on their offer of submitting rewrites. After two further attempts, they finally accepted my first book and I became a published author.

I'd love to say that my book shot to the top of the world's best seller lists, but sadly it didn't. However, my first book did manage to get onto the shelves of numerous high street shops and most importantly airport bookshops where I picked up quite a lot of sales from people who wanted a light read whilst laying on the beach. I managed to sell enough copies that I made what at the time seemed to me like a lot of money, but more importantly my publisher said they would publish my next book after I outlined the plot to them. The second book was distinctly more successful than the first as I now had a better idea of outline and structure, and having written eleven books, I decided I had made enough money to start considering what else I could do with my life.

On average it takes me about six months to write a book from scratch, and while I was working on my twelfth novel and considering what to do with my life, an old friend of mine asked me if I had ever considered becoming a magistrate as he thought I would be good at it. He pointed out that it was a voluntary role and was unpaid, although being a magistrate did cover all your expenses. My friend told me the Lord Chancellor's office, the government board that appointed all UK magistrates, were always looking for people who were 'prepared to serve' as they called it, were able to think clearly, and sum up all the evidence presented to them in an unbiased, calm and rational manner. To cut a long story short, the idea of becoming a magistrate really appealed to me, and after a series of lengthy interviews and several training courses, I was eventually appointed a magistrate or Justice of the Peace.

From then on I was entitled to put JP after my name, although in fact I never did use the initials as I always thought it sounded a bit pretentious.

I loved sitting on 'the bench' as they call it in the magistrate's court from day one, and I particularly liked the fact that you weren't up there on your own, but sat as a group of three. The most experienced magistrate always sat in the centre with he or she taking the lead as Chairman, and the Chairman was the only magistrate that could actually address the CPS or prosecution, the defence counsel and questioned all the various witnesses for both sides in court. However, as one of the two "side" magistrates, we were always able to ask any questions we may have had from witnesses via the Chairman. After all the evidence had been presented and all the various questions answered, the Chairman would often have a decision and a sentence in mind, and would frequently lean over to us and ask us if we concurred. We usually did, but quite often when it wasn't obvious, we'd "retire" to the magistrate's room behind the courtroom where we would sit and discuss the evidence over a cup of tea, sometimes calling in the "Clerk of the Court" who was the court's legally qualified expert. All three magistrates had been provided with a book of guidelines with the minimum and maximum sentences relating to all the various offences, but the "Clerk of the Court" ensured that the magistrates were always aware of what their legal options were, in case they were about to hand out an inappropriate sentence. But generally speaking, the final decision was always made by the three magistrates in agreement. I did do the occasional stint on my own however—always on a Saturday morning—but these sessions were simply what are known as remand hearings where I had to decide if the defendant was liable to do a runner, threaten a witness or try and bribe anyone. If I thought he or she was liable to do any of the above I would then remand them into custody, which usually meant they spent the rest of the weekend in the local prison until they were brought back to court on Monday morning for a full hearing in front of three magistrates.

Those days on the bench were some of the happiest I can recall, and I must say I learnt an awful lot about various offences, particularly lots of information on how the criminal mind works having seen it first hand in court. Needless to say, some of what I'd seen and heard in court crept into my books, but obviously the names and exact details were changed, not to protect the innocent however, but to stop me being either sued or pursued by angry criminals.

Then just under five years ago, my life changed completely. I was thirty three years old, had just about earned enough money from my crime novels to retire on—if I wanted to retire that young—but two things happened at more or less the same time. One, I realised that after roughly ten years, I was fed up with writing about crime, and two, I was starting to get pain in my fingers. I'd been a very amateur musician ever since I'd left school, but I really loved playing the piano, and even if I say so myself, I was reasonably talented. Using a chunk of money I'd made from my books, I'd treated myself to a brand new, rather nice, shiny, black, six-foot three-inch long Yamaha grand piano which took pride of place in the bay window of my second-floor flat in South London. I played most days, although mainly for my own amusement as I was still single. I'd had several girlfriends over the years, some serious, most not, but I'd never met "the one", although I was still hopeful. Anyway, back to my fingers.

I made an appointment with my local GP and he advised me that it could be the start of rheumatism or it might be arthritis, but whichever it was there wasn't much he could do to provide a cure. His helpful suggestion was that I went to live in a country with a much warmer and drier climate. I went back to my flat deep in thought, sat down and weighed up his suggestion over a cup of tea and a few bourbon biscuits. I much prefer tea over coffee, I always have and I suspect I always will, although I do drink coffee occasionally.

By my second cup of tea and my fourth bourbon biscuit, by the way in case you hadn't realised I really love bourbon biscuits—sorry, I digress—I had analysed my life in very rough detail and come to several conclusions; I was thirty three years old with no regular girlfriend, and at that moment in time I was definitely single. No ties to the UK there then. My parents had sadly died years earlier, and being an only child, I had no brothers or sisters—so no family ties either. As for my career—well I was a writer, and as long as I had my laptop and access to the internet for research—I could do that anywhere in the world. Thinking about it, I came to the conclusion that I loved the sun and I hated the drizzle, rain, storms, thunder, lightning, snow, hale, wind, mist, fog and all the other unpleasant weather conditions that England frequently throws at you. I decided the only thing I would really miss was being a magistrate, but that was not enough of a pull to keep me from leaving. So that was it—decision made—I would leave England behind, and go and live in the sun. The only question was…where?

I'd been very fortunate in that my writing had led me to research lots of various countries and cities around the world for detailed plot backgrounds. I seemed to recall somewhere that my writing hero Frederick Forsyth had once said, 'You can get a lot of detail about a country or a specific town or city from the internet, but nothing beats actually visiting the place and just walking the streets.' Anyway, that became my excuse when after my third novel became quite successful, my publisher had reluctantly agreed to subsidise my research trips, provided I didn't stay in glamorous five star hotels and that I only flew on bucket airlines if they were paying. So I had travelled to numerous corners of the world, and as a result I now had lots of possible places to consider. However, some I loved and some I absolutely hated. I loved the city of Salzburg in Austria when it was sunny, but that was sadly a complete non-starter as it rained there just as frequently as it did in England. I loved the beautiful perfume town of Grasse in the south of France, but unfortunately France is full of French people! I loved Munich, but my German was atrocious, and I knew I'd never get the hang of speaking the language. Also, quite frankly it always seems such an aggressive language. Anyway, my doctor had said that I needed sun and warmth, and to be perfectly honest I quite liked to idea of having daily access to a beach.

My mind immediately went to the Bahamas which I'd visited on a recent holiday, and I'd never seen clearer or bluer water in my life, and what's more, the water was really warm. But the Bahamas was also a very long way away, and as much as I'd enjoyed most of the Caribbean islands and numerous trips to different parts of America I had visited, I decided I couldn't live in either on a permanent basis. I liked visiting islands, but I could never live on one as I would feel trapped knowing I had to get either a boat or a plane anytime I wanted to go somewhere. Then there's the United States! To be honest, my main problem with North America is their crazy obsession with guns. A country where it is apparently quite normal for over 30,000 of their civilians to be shot dead every year by their fellow civilians cannot in my mind be called civilised, and I'm not making it up! The figures I've just quoted were recently published as a simple matter of fact article in the Seattle Times. Secondly, being ill in the United States can cost more than having a mortgage. As I said, crazy! Having quickly ruled out all of Asia, Australasia, Africa and South America simply because they were all too far from the UK—and I would need to visit the UK regularly as that was where my publisher is based—I decided my new home had to be somewhere in Europe. I immediately narrowed it down to a choice of the few countries lining the Mediterranean. I quickly ruled out all the various counties of North Africa such as Morocco. Tunisia, Libya, Algeria, Egypt etc. as none of them really appealed, and I guess the obvious choice for most people would be Spain. But for me that wasn't the case as I knew that's where most of the UK's ex-pat criminals had gone after fleeing from the Britain's shores, and I'd had enough of criminals over the last ten years. France was a no-no as I said earlier—a very beautiful country, but unfortunately full of French people. Italy was another big no, as in my mind, it was still run by the Mafia, and Greece was also not an option because I like restaurants that serve simple food like steak and chips with a nice bottle of cold beer as the norm, not something I can't even pronounce with a bottle of Ouzo or Raki—both of which I personally think taste bloody awful. So where was left? The answer was simple, Portugal, and in particular the sunny Algarve.

Chapter Two

For those of you who know your geography, you're probably thinking 'but Portugal's not on the Med'. True, but I'd been to the Algarve several times on holiday, and on each occasion I'd loved it. If you're not familiar with the Algarve, it is the southern strip of coast that runs along the base of Portugal, which on a map is the lump of land to the left of Spain, and it is also the westernmost part of Europe. The Algarve is quite a small area and is roughly 120 miles East to West, and 30 miles North to South. It gets 300 plus days of sunshine a year, has really great beaches, great food, great beer, great wine, a fantastically low cost of living apart from the cost of cars, and some of the friendliest people in the world. So later that month, having made my decision and handing in my notice on my rented flat, I packed everything of both monetary and sentimental value, jumped on a plane from Gatwick to Faro with all my worldly possessions following on behind in the removal lorry, with the plan that everything was going into storage in an Algarve warehouse until I'd found myself a new home.

I thought I would rent somewhere for a few weeks while I looked for a property to buy, but five years later I'm still renting the same original villa I first moved into. I live in an area of the Algarve named Quinta do Lago, which—for anyone that knows the Algarve—is a complex of several very lush golf courses, some of the best in the world in fact. These wonderful golf courses are all surrounded by multi-million pound villas, beautifully manicured gardens and attractive lakes, making it some of the most expensive real estate on the planet. Now I have been extremely lucky in life and I have a reasonable amount of money in the bank from my book sales, but I'm by no means a multi-millionaire. When I first arrived in the Algarve, I had been fortunate enough to find a really good local estate agent who was also a property letting agent. He offered me a beautiful, modern three bedroom villa to rent from its wealthy owner who both lived and worked in Monaco. He'd only taken on the property two days earlier and said that the owner had bought the villa at Quinta do Lago straight from the drawing board and he was simply looking to receive a regular income from the property, which he then wanted to keep as a long term inheritance for his three children. I was more than happy to pay him what I considered to be a very reasonable rate for such a wonderful villa in the sun. Earlier this year, the lease on the villa was up, and both he and I were very happy to sign a new five year lease for slightly more money.

Shortly after settling in the Algarve, I flew back to London for a meeting with my publisher, and I explained to them that I didn't want to write crime thrillers anymore, but I still wanted to write, and more importantly, still write for them. As I enjoyed travelling so much, I wondered if they would be happy to publish my own unique version of travel books, in which I would also include details of both real and fictional crime locations people could visit, including details of the relevant crime that had taken place there, either for real or in a writers mind. I explained to my publisher that these books would be aimed particularly at the traveller who wants to do more on holiday than simply cover themselves in factor thirty and lie in the sun for two weeks. Fortunately my publisher loved the idea, and they have so far published four very successful travel books on Italy, France, Germany and Russia, now reproduced in eleven different languages.

After I had been in the Algarve a few weeks, I started getting quite bad headaches. I wasn't unduly concerned but I thought I better get it checked out. George, my next door neighbour had lived on Quinta do Lago for seven years, and he told me that by far the best doctor in the area was Sam Clark. Apparently Doctor Clark was now a private doctor and therefore quite expensive, but nevertheless very good. I made an appointment for the following day, and whilst sitting alone in the reception area, the receptionist, for lack of other patients to talk to, became very chatty and told me that before coming to the Algarve, Sam Clark had been a top GP in South London and had also worked as one of three police surgeons who were on permanent call whenever London's Metropolitan Police required their services. I was also told by the receptionist that Dr Clark was 36 years old and wasn't married. I had no idea why she would think I might be interested in the doctor's marital status, but that was only until I met my new doctor. Sam was in fact short for Samantha, who turned out to be an incredibly attractive lady with shoulder length blonde hair who looked to me a good ten years younger than her actual age. She had a fantastic figure and a smile to die for. I was totally besotted with her on site, but I tried hard to concentrate on my headaches rather than Sam's smile. My neighbour had been correct—Sam Clark was an excellent doctor and she discovered pretty quickly that my headaches were in fact being caused by me not always wearing my sun glasses when

I was out and about. Sam also told me that my old sun glasses that I'd brought with me were OK for the UK, where the sun comes out on average just three days a year (I do tend to exaggerate by the way), but she said they weren't really up to the job for the strength of the Algarve sun. So later that day, I drove into Almancil, the nearest town, and bought myself two new pairs of sunglasses with a much darker tint at the opticians Sam had recommended, and my headaches miraculously cleared up within days.

Sam and I next bumped into each other a few days later in a local coffee shop on the edge of one of Quinta do Lago's pristine golf courses, and we chatted for a good twenty minutes over coffee and rich chocolate cake in her case, and for me, tea and fabulous little custard tarts—a local Portuguese favourite I had now come to love—which you can get everywhere.

'It turned out that over the years, Sam had read all my crime thrillers, and she, alongside some of the Met's police officers she'd worked with, had often discussed my spurious plots and claimed that they would have always solved the crimes long before my fictional hero had. Sam and I really hit it off; we were both very relaxed in each other's company, and over the next weeks, months and years, we became extremely good friends. Sadly, me being the great romantic coward, I never approached the subject of going on a proper date with Sam in fear of spoiling our close friendship. To be honest, I'm still totally besotted with her, and I hope to one day pluck up the courage to tell her how I really feel—but that definitely won't be today.

Chapter Three

Well I think that just about brings you up to date.

It was 8:30 on Monday morning, and I was having a quiet mug of tea and a few of my favourite bourbon biscuits while sitting outside in the early morning sun in just a pair of shorts and my flip-flops. Sitting by the pool at the back of the villa is something I find very pleasant and really relaxing and this Monday morning was no exception—at least, it wasn't until the front doorbell rang. I got up, went through the villa and answered the door to discover it was my gardener and his wife. They come twice a week, every week and mow the grass, trim the hedges, weed the flower beds, clean the pool and do whatever else it is that gardeners do! Their names are Andrei and Cristina and they are both Romanian in their early thirties. They are a lovely couple and they are as honest as they come. They both work really hard and are extremely conscientious in their work in the garden every Tuesday and Friday morning. But as I said—today was Monday.

'Hi,' I said. 'I thought you weren't due here until tomorrow?'

'No we aren't,' replied Andrei. 'It's not about the garden. Can we please talk to you about something very important? We are really worried about our friend.'

'Of course,' I replied and invited them into the villa.

The three of us sat down in the main lounge and Andrei started speaking.

'It's about our neighbour and good friend Alexandru. He's been arrested by the GNR for murder. We have known Alexandru for many years and I promise you Mr Michael, he would not do this terrible thing.'

GNR is the shorthand used by everyone in Portugal for the police. In fact it actually stands for "Guarda Nacional Republicana" which in English translates as the National Republican Guard. It is the GNR that are mostly seen in Portugal and they are usually the starting point for all crimes committed in Portugal. There is also a second force known as the "Policia de Segurança Pública" or the "Public Security Police". They are a civilian police force who work mainly in the larger urban areas such as Lisbon and Porto. Then there is the "Policia Judiciária" or the "Judicial Police". The "PJ" are overseen by the Public Ministry, they investigate all the larger cases, and if the "PJ" get involved, then you really are in trouble. Last but by no means least, there is the "Polícia Marítima". I feel no explanation is needed as I think the name speaks for itself—even in Portuguese!

'I'm always happy to help you or your friends Andrei as you know,' I responded, 'but I'm not sure what I can do, and why would you think I can help you with this anyway.'

'You must know lots of important people, Mr Michael. You were a judge in England and you've written all those murder books—you are a crime expert and can help my friend. You also know him, he has helped us with your garden several times.' To be honest I didn't remember Alexandru at all, but now wasn't the time to mention it.

'Firstly Andrei, I wasn't a judge. I was just a magistrate and that is very different, and secondly I'm not a crime expert. All those books I wrote were just stories I'd invented.'

'But you will still help us, yes?' pleaded Cristina. 'We know Alexandru and he wouldn't do this thing.'

'Tell me,' I asked, 'why do the GNR think it is Alexandru that murdered this person, and who is it that he has supposedly murdered?' I soon wished I hadn't asked.

'It is Mr Malcolm Tisbury,' Andrei replied.

'Malcolm, from three doors away?' I asked. I had known Malcolm ever since I moved to Quinta do Lago five years ago, and I regarded him as a friend—not a close friend, but more than just an acquaintance.

'Yes, Mr Malcolm. He was stabbed to death in the chest, and his throat was cut,' confirmed Cristina.

'And why on earth do the GNR think your friend Alexandru did this horrible thing?' I asked.

'Because written in blood on the wall of the lounge in our Romanian language was the message 'Die engleză milionar de porc' which means "Die English Millionaire Pig", and it was written using Mr Malcolm's blood,' said Cristina.

'Also,' said Andrei, 'lying on the floor next to Mr Malcolm's body was Alexandru's gardening knife—covered in Mr Malcom's blood.'

The main entrance of the Conrad Hotel, Quinta do Lago

Michael and Sam's villa at Quinta do Lago

One of the many golf courses at Quinta do Lago

The beach near Quinta do Lago

Chapter Four

I was both shocked and puzzled in equal measure by what I'd just heard. Malcolm had been a neighbour, a good neighbour at that for over five years, and it was a shock to realise he was dead. But at the same time, I couldn't imagine anyone being stupid enough to write a message in their own foreign language, and even more so to leave the murder weapon lying on the floor next to the body. If this was a novel and not real life I would not believe that Andrei was guilty for a second, and that he was being set up. But this wasn't a novel, it was real life, and I needed to talk it through with someone.

I told Andrei and Cristina that I would do my best to help and showed them out of the villa, promising to keep in touch, and then I got dressed. It was going to be another warm day in the Algarve, so I just put on a pair of beige slacks, a plain blue tee shirt and a pair of slip on dark blue leather boat shoes which I always found to be very comfortable. I jumped into my car, a Jaguar XF in Italian racing red with a very smart ivory leather interior, and headed off to Sam's surgery which was just a short five minute drive. The new Jag was one of my few luxuries, but I loved it and to hell with the cost. Cars are extremely expensive in Portugal, sometimes even double the cost of the same car if bought in England, but the steering wheel of English bought cars is on the wrong side. Also, if you happen to be driving a non-Portuguese car you will undoubtedly get stopped fairly regularly by the GNR, and you will then spend half your life lying that you are on holiday and therefore the crazy Portuguese laws on cars don't apply to you. The trouble is, most of the GNR now know me and they also know where I live, so I can't use that excuse. I just wanted an easy life, so I thought to hell with it and bought a brand new XF, all built to my own spec, from the local Jaguar dealer in Faro.

I arrived at Sam's surgery to discover a fairly new dark blue Range Rover sitting outside parked next to Sam's car and her receptionist's old silver Volkswagen Polo. Sam had bought her car, a two year old white Mercedes C Class Sport, last year from a patient who was returning to the UK to live, and no longer wanted a left hand drive vehicle. Sam absolutely loved it, although I much preferred my nice new Jag and frequently told her so. Sam's receptionist was a 28 year old young lady named Jan Cochrane, and like most of us who either lived or worked at Quinta do Lago, Jan was also British. Sam frequently told me that Jan was very efficient, ran the surgery extremely well and that Sam's business probably wouldn't survive without Jan's brilliant admin skills. However, the Range Rover parked outside probably meant Sam had a client in the surgery and so I got ready for a long wait. In fact the wait was only about 5 minutes when a couple who I estimated to be in their mid to late sixties emerged from Sam's consulting room. They thanked Sam profusely for her ongoing help and then went over to see Jan to make another appointment for the following month. I jumped in straight away and walked straight into the consulting room without saying a word.

'Good morning to you too, Michael,' said Sam sarcastically as she followed me into the consulting room and closed the door behind her. 'Please come in—oh, I'm sorry, I see you have already.'

'Sorry Sam, and good morning. I didn't mean to be rude, but my mind is all over the place. I've just discovered Malcolm Tisbury, one of my neighbours, was murdered last night, and I wanted to talk to you about it. My gardener's friend has been accused of the murder and he has been arrested by the GNR. My gardener and his wife are both convinced he's innocent and they've asked me if I can help.'

'God Michael, I thought I'd left murder and mayhem behind when I resigned as a police surgeon and left London. Tell me, what happened, well as far as you can anyway.' So I disclosed everything I knew to Sam, which in all honesty wasn't that much, including my initial thoughts that it sounded to me like a massive set up.

'I agree with you, Michael,' said a thoughtful Sam, 'it's far too obvious, but knowing them and how they think, or in their case don't, it may not be quite so obvious to the GNR.' The GNR sadly have a terrible reputation across Europe for not being the sharpest knives in the box after the fiasco of their lengthy and non-productive investigation into the Madeline McCann kidnapping many years earlier. It's not true though; the GNR are normally quite good.

'I assume the killer was after diamonds?' asked Sam.

'Why would you assume that, and what diamonds?' I asked. I didn't want to appear stupid, but I had a feeling I was about to.

'Well, I would have thought it was obvious,' said Sam, 'with Malcolm being a diamond dealer. I know his offices were in London's Hatton Garden and I do know he often had uncut diamonds in the safe at his villa. Have the GNR checked the safe?'

'Malcolm was one of my neighbours for five years,' I responded, 'and I had no idea he was a diamond dealer. How the hell did you know, and how on earth would you know he kept uncut diamonds at the villa?'

'Simple,' replied Sam, 'I was his doctor, and patients tell their doctors all sorts of private and personal things they don't tell other people. I only looked after Malcolm for the last couple of years when he came to me worried about what he thought might have been a slight heart attack scare. We talked about the possible stresses and strains in his life, and what he did for a living. It came out during our conversation that as a diamond dealer and jeweller, he occasionally kept uncut diamonds in his safe, a stress he was quite concerned about. Of course I wouldn't normally break the doctor/patient confidentiality rule, but I'm only telling you this now because poor Malcolm is dead, he has no wife or kids and lastly, it might be helpful.'

'Wow!' I stuttered. 'So what do we do now?' I asked, not really expecting an answer. 'I don't suppose there's any chance you can shut up shop while we figure out if there's anything we can do to help?'

'There's every chance. As it happens, today is very quiet. I only have one patient due in here later this morning for a routine appointment, and I can get Jan to move them to next week. I wasn't going to be working this afternoon anyway.'

'Great. So I repeat my question—what do we do?'

'Well I suggest we go and see Inspector Paulo Cabrita. He heads up the Almancil GNR station. He would initially be in charge of any incident or crime that takes place in his area, and Quinta do Lago falls under his area.'

'It sounds like you know him.'

'Only by reputation, which incidentally is very good. People that know him say he is not very GNR like, and believe me, that is a compliment. He's risen through the ranks quite quickly by using his brain. If I remember rightly he's only 34, has a wife and two young daughters.'

'And how on earth do you know all that if you've never met him,' I stupidly asked.

'Same as before, his wife brought the girls to the surgery last year when Katrina—the eldest—fell out of a tree in the garden and broke her arm. We got chatting and talked briefly about her husband before I sent them off to Faro hospital.'

'So in fact, being a doctor is actually the best way of finding out all the local gossip on everyone?' I asked.

'Oh yes, definitely, but bear in mind—as a doctor I can't really repeat anything. Well not the juicy stuff anyway, so it can be very frustrating as sometimes you hear things you'd love to repeat—but you never can. Right, I'll get Jan to move my other appointment, and then we can head into Almancil. I assume we're going in your car as you always refuse to travel in mine?'

'Of course. Why on earth would I want to travel in your tatty old second hand transport when I have a brand new and far superior luxury vehicle at my disposal?' I replied remembering to duck as Sam picked up a paperback book from her desk and threw it at my head. We seemed to spend half our lives jokingly slagging off each other's cars, knowing full well that they were both in fact excellent vehicles. I just preferred mine.

Chapter Five

GNR Inspector Paulo Cabrita was in his office and fortunately for us he had been put in charge of the initial enquiry into the murder of Malcolm Tisbury. He invited us into his office, mainly because he knew of Sam through his wife and Katrina's accident. We went through the preliminary introductions, the fact that Malcolm was a neighbour and that in our combined humble opinion, this was a massive set up.

'Inspector Cabrita…' I began.

'Please,' he interrupted, 'call me Paulo. I have a feeling we will be having many conversations over the coming weeks, and I hate formality.'

'Paulo, I am a writer and I used to be a crime writer, and over the years I have written several murder mysteries, and to me—and Sam here agrees, this sounds far too obvious a set up to deliberately try and put the blame on someone else. I just can't believe it to be true.'

'As it happens, I am quite familiar with your books, Mr Michael,' replied Paulo.

The Portuguese have a habit of using your Christian name and then putting Mr in front of it, and the Inspector was no exception.

'I have in fact read several of them, although personally speaking I think I would have found the criminals far quicker than your hero does. Though, if I'm honest I can't say the same of some of my colleagues. As far as this case is concerned however, let me start by saying that I agree with you that this looks like a set up to put the blame on somebody else.'

'Great,' said Sam, 'so can Alexandru be released on bail?'

'No, I'm afraid not,' replied Paulo. 'There is this annoying little thing we have to deal with called evidence, and as far as the GNR are concerned—all the evidence points to Mr Alexandru Dumitrescu. As much as I'd like to, I cannot bail him until I have some concrete evidence that indicates he didn't do it!'

'I'm sorry to ask this Paulo,' I queried, 'but are the GNR actually looking for someone else, or are they happy to simply go with the obvious?'

'I know the GNR sadly have a reputation for always settling for the easy option,' replied Paulo, 'but I assure you I am not like that, and I will be doing all I can to find the real murderer. Look, Mr Michael, if you think you can help then I would be most grateful for any information you might have or for that matter anything you and Miss Sam can do to help, but it cannot be made general knowledge that I am sharing information with you.'

Paulo reached into the large central door of his desk and pulled out a folder.

'These are the photographs my officers took at the scene this morning, and it is not what you call a pretty site. I will show them to you now, and before you ask, no, you cannot have copies.'

There were about fifteen photographs, all ten by eight and in glorious technicolour, and they were all pretty gruesome. Malcolm had been stabbed several times in the chest, and his throat had also been cut. But not with the usual straightforward slicing movement as I had expected. Instead, his throat had been cut about a dozen times with numerous zigzag stabbing cuts so that it looked like it had been attacked with a pair of dressmaker's pinking shears. As Paulo said, it was not a pretty site.

Sam hadn't said a word after we had looked through the photographs, but then she gently poked me in the ribs with her elbow as she said:

'Thank you, Paulo, it was very generous of you to show us the pictures. If we have any ideas or anything useful to contribute we will get in touch with you personally.'

'But Sam…' I started to say as I had more questions, but then I received another elbow in the stomach for my trouble. It was then that I realised I needed to shut up.

'Do you have a card with your mobile number on it?' Sam asked Paulo as she stood up ready to leave. Paulo reached into his jacket pocket and handed us both one of his business cards.

'Thank you for coming to see me,' said Paulo, 'and please let me know if you have any thoughts or ideas that may help the case.'

'Of course,' replied Sam.

We all shook hands and then left the GNR station. Sam still hadn't said a word and she was obviously deep in thought, so following her lead I kept quiet until we were seated in my car and starting to head back to the villa that I asked the question on my mind.

'What the hell was all that about Sam, and if you keep elbowing me in the ribs like that I'll have to go and see a really good doctor, and I'm pretty sure it won't be you.'

'I know who murdered Malcolm,' said Sam very quietly.

'You what?' I exclaimed, jamming on the brakes and causing the car behind me to swerve into the middle of the road and honking me several times whilst making very rude gestures out of his side window.

'I know who murdered Malcolm,' repeated Sam. 'Can you please drop me off at the surgery so that I can pick up my car, go home and pack a bag, and then I'll meet you back at yours in half an hour or so. I don't want to say anything more at the moment, but please, just trust me. Go home, pack a bag for a few days, and for goodness sake please don't forget your passport and your credit cards—we need to get to London as soon as possible. Oh, and by the way, you got me into this mess, so you're paying.'

Chapter Six

I dropped Sam off at the surgery as requested, and she was back at my house twenty five minutes later. I'd packed a bag as she'd requested and was ready to leave when Sam got to my front door and entered the villa.

'I've spoken to Jan and she is cancelling all my appointments for the rest of the week. I'm sorry for all the mystery Michael, and the rush, but I wanted to get everything clear in my head before I filled you in.'

'First question,' I said. 'You told me earlier that you knew who had murdered Malcolm. Who was it, and why didn't you just tell Paulo and let him deal with it?'

'To answer your question, I know who did it because I've seen his handiwork before, when I was a police surgeon, but I can't for the life of me remember his name. That's why we're going to London. We're going to see Detective Sergeant Paul Naismith, at least I assume he's still a DS. He and I worked together quite a bit when we were both based at Greenwich Police Station in South London, and Paul should have all the old files we'll need to refer to.'

As Sam was talking, I set the villa's alarm, locked the front door behind us, and dumped both our bags on the back seat of the car. We climbed into the Jag and headed to Faro airport where I parked the car in one of the long stay car parks.

Faro is not massive as international airports go, but it does have several different airlines offering regular flights to London. During the summer EasyJet have several flights going to Gatwick every day, and Ryanair fly daily to London Stansted, which is actually nowhere near London, but the best route from our point of view would be to get a flight with British Airways who fly directly into London City airport. We were lucky, as BA's lunchtime flight had plenty of space on it, and three hundred euros later we had two boarding passes. The flight to London was pleasant enough and only took just over two and a quarter hours. After clearing customs, we hired a small car and drove across South London to Greenwich. It felt strange being back in South London where I'd lived most of my life. I knew Greenwich quite well, and I'd even done some research for one of my early novels with a couple of policemen on the night shift at Westcombe Park Police station which was just down the road from Greenwich. We entered the building and immediately Sam was recognised by several of the officers. One even recognised me.

'Hi George,' said Sam to the desk Sergeant on duty. 'Is DS Naismith on duty and by any chance available for a chat?'

'Hello Sam, good to see you again,' said the Sergeant. 'As it happens, DS Naismith is now DI Naismith,' said the sergeant as he picked up the phone.

'Hi Paul. There is an extremely attractive young lady in reception asking for you by name, and she wondered if you could spare her a minute of your most valuable time?'

Paul Naismith obviously replied with some comment or other and the Sergeant merely said:

'You'll have to ask her that yourself,' and put the phone down.

Thirty seconds later Detective Inspector Paul Naismith walked through the door from the back of the station and into the reception area. He was about five foot ten inches tall, and had what I would describe as a mop of floppy blonde hair.

'Good grief—Dr Samantha Clarke as I live and breathe—well at least I now know the answer to my question is the former and not the latter.'

Paul walked forward and gave Sam a big hug and shook hands with me. 'I asked George if the attractive young lady in reception was after my brain, or was it my amazing body she wanted. Sadly in all the years I've known you it was always my mind and never my perfectly formed body you wanted.'

'Oh you know me so well, Paul,' smiled Sam, and turning to me she said, 'this is a colleague and really good friend of mine from the Algarve, the novelist Michael Turner.'

'Hi, I thought I recognised your face, but I couldn't put a name to it. It's nice to meet you, and yes before you ask, I have read all your books, although I have to say I thought I could have solved the murders long before your detective ever did.' Sam just smiled as she looked at the floor.

'You know, the next person that says that I'm going to hit very hard.' I was feeling quite indignant on behalf of my hero who was now appearing to be a bit slow.

'Well, well, well' came a voice from behind us. 'If that's not Sam Clarke's beautifully proportioned backside then I'm not Superintendent Stephen Colshaw.' Sam smiled as she turned round and gave the Superintendent a hug.

'You know, Stephen, you really are the ugliest Superintendent in this police station.'

'True,' he replied, 'but as you well know, I am also the only Superintendent in this police station, so that means I'm also by far the most handsome.'

Actually he was quite good looking and obviously had a good sense of humour. Sam introduced me again and then surprise, surprise, Superintendent Colshaw said the same thing.

'I loved your books, Michael, but to be perfectly honest I thought your detective was sometimes a bit slow in solving the crimes.'

As he said it, both Sam and Paul took a step back and just stared at me.

I just smiled back and said, 'Superintendents don't count.'

They both laughed, and Sam told him how I'd threatened to thump the next person to ridicule the crime solving expertise of my fictional hero. Everyone laughed.

'If you don't mind me asking, Sam, what on earth are you doing back here?'

'Well I was hoping to pick Paul's brains about an old case we both worked on, and I think the bastard's just committed a similar murder in our part of the world.'

'In that case, Paul, give Sam every bit of help you can—and that's an order. Well I'm afraid you'll have to forgive me, Sam, you too Michael, but I must be getting on. I'll love you and leave you as they say. You know what it's like for us Superintendents—I've got this really exciting budget meeting to get to and I can't wait. Bye Sam, and great to see you again. I hope you find your man.' And with that Superintendent Colshaw left.

'Come through to my office, Sam, you too, Michael, and let's see how I can help.'

DI Paul Naismith shared an office with his DS, but he was out and so we had the place to ourselves. Sam immediately got down to work.

‘Do you remember a series of murders about five years or more ago Paul, just before I stopped working as a Police Surgeon? The murderer had a way of cutting his victim’s throats so that it looked like they’d been attacked with a pair of pinking shears. We were sure we knew who it was, but we could never get our hands on him.’

‘Oh I remember him alright. Freddie Drayton!’

‘Yes!’ exclaimed Sam in a triumphant voice, ‘that was him. Didn’t he work for some big crime lord for want of a better term? I don’t remember names as I didn’t really get involved in the cases, just the medical side, but I do remember his name now you’ve said it.’

‘Do you have any information on him Paul?’ I asked.

‘Hang on a sec,’ said Paul, ‘I’ll go and dig out the old files for you, and then you can have photocopies of anything you think may be useful.’

‘Will that be OK?’ I asked. ‘We’re not police officers.’

‘Of course,’ replied Paul, ‘the Super ordered me to help you in any way I can didn’t he? And I’m not going to go against the Superintendent’s orders. Besides, I assume you’re going to be heading back to the Algarve and taking any copies I give you with you, so what the Super doesn’t know can’t hurt him, or even more importantly, hurt me.’

‘Thanks Paul,’ I said as he headed out the door.

It was nearly a quarter of an hour before Paul got back, but he had several thick files with him. The three of us then sat down around a table next to Paul’s desk.

‘Right,’ said Paul opening up the first file, ‘according to my files Freddie Drayton will now be 52 years old, and he was the full time enforcer for Derek Clive Simpson, who is a another really nasty bit of work. We’re pretty sure Simpson was the main instigator and brains behind several of Europe’s leading jewel heists, but we could never prove anything—basically Simpson was a very successful diamond thief.

'You keep saying "was", Paul, does that mean Drayton and Simpson are out of the business and retired, or are they still around?' I asked.

'To be honest, Michael, we have no idea. Simpson and his gang operated for about ten years in the UK and mostly in our manor, so we got to know him quite well. We estimate he'd nicked at least ten million pounds worth of diamonds and emeralds over that time, and in the process had two diamond dealers, and half a dozen staff of various London jewellery shops murdered. Sadly we could never prove anything, even though we were sure it was him. Simpson always had a very expensive lawyer on permanent speed dial. Towards the end of that period we'd managed to tie him into a very nasty robbery and murder in Hatton Garden, but as we were getting close to nabbing him, he and the gang all flitted the country. We know they initially went to Marbella on the Costa del Crime, but then they just disappeared.'

'Who exactly was in the gang?' I asked.

Paul reached for another folder, pulled out and spread six head and shoulder full colour photographs on the table. He pointed to each one as he spoke.

'This guy is Derek Clive Simpson, and he is the brains of the operation. He's a clever bugger when it comes to thieving, and he never does any of the dirty work himself. He always ensures he has a cast iron alibi for the time of the crime. You know the sort of thing, him and his wife dining with friends at a restaurant, or drinking with a crowd of people at a club. Anything and anywhere he can be seen and positively identified by both clients and staff so that we can't accuse him of being at any of the crime scenes. He usually chose posh restaurants that used CCTV inside the restaurant as well as outside, knowing full well it would provide even stronger proof that he was nowhere near the scene at the time.

'Do you think they're still in Spain?' asked Sam.

'God knows,' replied Paul. 'It's a bloody massive country and because of the never ending feud over Gibraltar, the sodding Spanish aren't that keen on helping the British police, so it's the ideal country to hide out in. But if I had to bet on it though, yeah, I'd say they were still holed up somewhere in Spain.'

'You know, Sam, the Algarve is only a three to four hour drive from Marbella,' I said. 'They could easily drive across the border, kill Malcolm, nick his uncut diamonds, assuming that's what was stolen, and then nip back over the border. They'd be well out of Portuguese jurisdiction and in another country before the Portuguese police even knew a crime had been committed.'

'I was thinking much the same,' said Sam. 'It's the perfect set up.'

'This,' said Paul pointing at the second photograph, 'is the lovely Sandra Simpson—Derek's trophy wife. She looks lovely and you'd never think anything nasty of her until you got to know her. She's a real nasty bitch, swears like a trooper, and the only people she was ever nice to were Derek and the rest of the gang.'

'She sounds lovely,' mused Sam.

'Freddie Drayton,' said Paul pointing at the third picture. 'We know for a fact that he has killed at least four people, and we are pretty sure we can lay another six murders at his door. He has almost a trademark that for some reason he does to all his victims—you mentioned it earlier in that he carves diagonal patterns in the neck of his victims. God knows why he does it—it's almost like advertising. Look! I've murdered another one. This was one of his victims six years ago,' said Paul pulling out another picture from a different folder and laying it on the table.

'That's identical to what he did to Malcolm,' I said, now totally convinced that Freddie Drayton was the murderer of my friend Malcolm.

'Keeping going,' said Paul, 'this is Jimmy Priestly, who is in theory Derek's chauffer, but in reality he is the getaway driver, and a bloody good one at that. Don't be fooled because he looks so young. He's only thirty one now, but he started hot wiring and nicking cars when he was only fourteen.' Pointing at the fifth photograph, Paul continued, 'This lovely charmer is the additional muscle that Freddie usually takes on jobs with him when he expects a bit of opposition. His name is Alex Donovan and he is basically just a giant hunk of thick Scottish lard. In lots of ways he's the gang's weak link. My goldfish has more brain cells than Alex Donavan, but he just blindly does whatever Freddie tells him to do, and Freddie just does whatever Derek tells him to do. I could never prove it of course, but I suspect Derek just does whatever Sandra tells him to do.'

'Who's that in the sixth photograph?' I asked.

'Ah, that is Mr Dominic St Clair, Derek Simpson's tame lawyer. He goes wherever Derek goes, and he was always on hand if we ever happened to call on Derek or Sandra. Dominic works exclusively with, or should I say works exclusively for serious criminals, and if the Simpson gang have all gone to Spain then you can be pretty sure Dominic St Clair will be somewhere close by.'

'So,' started Sam, 'we're pretty sure Malcolm's murder was committed by Freddie Drayton, probably under the orders of Derek Clive Simpson, and that the motive was getting their hands on a pile of uncut diamonds we think Malcolm had in his home safe.'

'The trouble is,' I said, 'firstly we don't really know where to start looking other than Marbella, but they may well have moved on from there anything up to five years ago, and secondly, at this stage we don't know if there were any uncut diamonds in Malcolm's safe to start with.'

'Would you like copies of these six photographs,' asked Paul, 'and is there anything else you think I can help with, bearing in mind we lost track of the gang five years ago?'

'No, I think that's all at the moment,' I said, 'and yes please re the photos, can we have two sets if possible. Thinking about it, I guess the next logical step is to go to Malcolm's office in Hatton Garden. His staff may well be able to help, or at least confirm if he did or didn't have stones at home.'

'That makes sense,' said Sam. 'I guess after Hatton Garden we go home to the Algarve, and then perhaps consider poking around in Marbella.'

'Well at least we now know who we're looking for,' I said.

Paul left the room with all the files and returned a few minutes later with two large brown envelopes, each of which contained seven large colour photographs—one of each of the five gang members, one of the lawyer and one of the close up of Freddie Drayton's handiwork. Paul handed us an envelope each, and he also gave Sam one of his business cards.

'Bye Sam, and for God's sake be careful,' said Paul. 'I'd hate to see Freddie Drayton going to work on that pretty neck of yours. Michael, I'm putting you in charge of looking after her. She's very precious to all of us here.'

'She's pretty precious to me as well,' I said, and then I realised I'd just said it out loud for Sam to hear as well. She just smiled at me but didn't say a word.

'You've got my number,' said Paul, 'and ring me anytime if you think I can help.'

Paul gave Sam a long hug, shook my hand firmly and then escorted us out of the building.

Greenwich Park, London

Greenwich Police Station, London

Greenwich Railway Station, London

The intercontinental hotel at the O2, London

Chapter Seven

We climbed back into our hire car, and after consulting the underground map headed for the car park at Greenwich Railway Station—all of five hundred yards away. We parked the car in the small station car park and got the next train from Greenwich into London Bridge, and then changed platforms in order to get the next train to Cannon Street, from where it was only a short walk across town to Hatton Garden. We'd come to the conclusion that trying to park a car in central London, even one as small as our hire car was going to be a complete non-starter, and we also quite liked the idea of having a train ride as neither of us had been on a train for five years. It was also a sunny day and we quite liked the idea of stretching our legs.

'I've just realised' said Sam, 'Malcolm's body was only found early this morning. God, that was only seven hours ago. His staff at the shop may not even know he's dead.'

'You're right,' I replied, 'it was only seven hours ago. We seem to have achieved a hell of a lot in such a short space of time. I guess all we can do is walk into the shop and try and get a feel for what they know.' And that's just what we did.

From what we could see on entering the shop, Malcolm mainly sold diamond based items, with a few emeralds, rubies and sapphires used to add a bit of colour to the more spectacular pieces. There were three staff behind the counters, two young ladies and a man about my age, plus a uniformed security man. It was pretty obvious from the moment we walked through the door that they had heard the sad news. The man came to greet us and introduced himself as Jeremy Green, the Manager.

'Good morning, Mr Green,' I began. 'My name is Michael Turner, and this is my colleague Dr Samantha Clarke. We've just flown in from the Algarve and it is obvious you've heard the sad news about Malcolm. He was my neighbour and my friend.'

'Indeed we have, Mr Turner—a very sad day for all of us. However, I'm sure you didn't come all this way to offer us your condolences, and I don't wish to appear rude, but what can we do for you?'

'We've just come from a lengthy meeting with the police in South London, and we had an earlier meeting this morning with the Portuguese police. We are all wondering if you can help us with a question no one else can answer.'

'Well if I can, I will. What is your question?'

'We know from previous conversations with Malcolm,' said Sam taking over, 'that he often had uncut stones in the safe at his villa in Portugal, but the police have no idea if there were any in there when the murderers broke in. They are wondering if that was the reason for the murder. You know, a robbery gone wrong when perhaps Malcolm disturbed them.'

'I assume from your question Doctor Clarke that no stones were found in the safe?'

'No, the safe was empty and left unlocked.'

'What I can tell you is that there should have been approximately two and a half million pounds worth of uncut diamonds sitting in Malcolm's safe. They arrived with him on

Friday via Pieter Van Straaten, our usual courier from De Beers who is our regular supplier of uncut stones in South Africa. Malcolm was going to sort and grade the stones over the weekend before the same courier was due to collect them on Tuesday, tomorrow that is, and take them to Amsterdam for cutting, polishing and mounting. They would then come here a few weeks later to the shop for display and sale. When finished, those stones would have had a potential retail value in excess of ten million pounds and they were the largest consignment Malcolm had ever had in his safe.'

'The obvious question then, Mr Green, is, who else knew about the stones, and how often did Malcolm have such deliveries?'

'Obviously Malcolm knew, and I knew. Nobody else here in the shop knew and again obviously the courier company knew as they arranged the delivery, and the cutters in Amsterdam knew to expect the stones tomorrow. As for was this normal? No, far from it. A quantity of stones like that was only shipped two or three times a year.'

'Thank you so much for your help, Mr Green,' said Sam, 'you've answered so many of our questions.'

'Well to be honest, Doctor Clarke, I've only told you things you could have easily found out for yourself anyway.'

'Nevertheless,' said Sam, 'we're so sorry to have disturbed you on such a difficult day. Will you keep trading and just out of interest, who now owns the company?'

'All I know is it's not me,' Green replied. 'I am simply the Manager, although I worked with Malcolm for over eleven years. Yes, I will keep the shop open and trade as normally as we can until whoever the new owner is tells me differently.'

'Once again, thank you, Mr Green,' I said, and with that Sam and I left the shop.

On the train back to Greenwich, Sam and I both felt Jeremy Green had been a bit shifty, but nothing we could really put our finger on. We chatted over what we had learned, but only after we had telephoned Inspector Paulo Cabrita back in Almancil to inform him of the missing two and half million pounds worth of uncut diamonds. Sam and I both felt that we knew pretty much what had happened. We had come to the obvious conclusion, well at least it seemed obvious to us, that Derek Simpson and his gang had driven from Spain into Portugal, had broken into Malcolm's during the night, committed the robbery, and in the process poor Malcolm had disturbed them and got himself killed. Freddie Drayton had tried to put the blame for the murder on a local Romanian workman, and then they'd all driven back over the border to their hidey-hole in Spain. What also seemed obvious to both of us was that they didn't hit on the idea of breaking into Malcolm's by chance. They must have known the stones would be there, and that meant they had inside information. All great in theory, but two slight problems. One, we had absolutely no evidence whatsoever, and two, we hadn't a clue where the Spanish hidey-hole might be other than Marbella. We talked it through and decided the first thing we had to do was to find out where their information came from, and in all probability that meant South Africa.

'You know, Michael, if we keep following this through it's going to get pretty expensive. We may even have to go to South Africa—I'm not saying we shouldn't go if we have to, but how do you feel about this. You don't even know who Alexandru is?'

'It's not about Alexandru,' I replied. 'It's about Malcolm and finding his killer. Yes, that may mean trips to Spain, Amsterdam and yes, even South Africa. But if it means we find Derek Simpson and his gang, and more importantly Freddie Drayton, and then help the authorities put him behind bars then it will be worth every penny. If you have no objection and can spare the time I want to keep going.'

'That's what I love about you—your determination and your honesty,' said Sam.

'Did you just use the word love?' I asked, trying to sound unemotional about it, although my heart was suddenly racing ninety to the dozen.

Sam was quiet and obviously deep in thought for about fifteen seconds, and then she said, 'Yes, Michael, I did say love. And don't tell me you don't feel the same way about me. I heard your "precious" comment about me earlier at the police station and I suppose it brought it home to me. I love you to bits you daft sod, and I have done for years, but sadly you're very much like me in that respect. We're both a pair of emotional cowards. I guess I knew all along that you were never going to bring the subject up, so I thought I'd better say something while I had the courage.'

'Wow' was all I could muster.

'Right,' said Sam. 'If we are going to do this and follow through, then I guess we'd better get moving and yes, before you ask I'm talking about both the murder and us. It's getting late, so let's stay in London overnight, have a decent meal, chat about what to do next and where on earth we go next.'

'I suppose I better book us into a hotel then,' I suggested. 'Um, Sam?'

'What now Michael?'

'Do I book one room or two?'

'Michael—I've just told you I love you. Which do you think?'

So I booked a double. In fact I booked a large suite. I was on cloud nine—the woman I have been in love with for the last few years had just told me she loved me too. And Sam was right, if it had been left to me I'd probably have been far too scared to say anything—ever. We had a great meal in the hotel's excellent dining room, during which we talked quite a bit about our relationship, how it had suddenly changed and where it was heading now that our feelings were out in the open. We then changed the subject back to Malcolm's murder, resolved what we could and couldn't do about trying to help solve it, where we were possibly going next, and then we finally headed for the lift and the suite. However, as far as the next few hours were concerned, I knew exactly what I was going to be doing next.

Chapter Eight

I woke feeling ten years younger, although I was actually completely exhausted. We'd had a wonderful night, but we were now ready to face a new day. We worked out a plan over breakfast, and decided part one was to get back to the Algarve and try and convince Paulo to release his prisoner in view of the new evidence. I booked two seats on an Easy Jet flight to Faro using my iPad and a credit card, as the British Airways flight wasn't until the evening and we didn't want to hang around doing nothing. So we drove down to Gatwick and returned the hire car.

The Tuesday afternoon flight back to Faro was uneventful. We picked up my Jag from the airport car park and decided to go straight to Almancil Police headquarters. Fortunately Paulo Cabrita was in his office and welcomed us with open arms—literally.

'Am I glad to see you two,' he started. 'Please, come through to my office and tell me everything you've found out, but first, would you like some coffee?'

One of the first things I learnt about the Portuguese is that they don't do anything without drinking coffee. Usually most Portuguese will drink an "espresso", which is a tiny cup of very strong black coffee, which to be perfectly honest I can't stand, so I asked for a "galão", which is usually served in a tall glass and is roughly a quarter black coffee and three quarters hot milk. Not very Portuguese—but it's how I like my coffee, and Sam asked for a standard "meia de leite", which is a standard white coffee in a standard cup and saucer. Having acted as our personal barista, Paulo sat down behind his desk and we went through everything we had learnt in both Greenwich and Hatton Garden, in the process showing him the photographs of the gang and the photo of Freddie Drayton's handiwork.

'It seems to us, Paulo,' I started, 'that without any shadow of a doubt, this crime was principally to steal two and a half million pounds worth of uncut diamonds. At today's exchange rate, that is roughly three million euros. We also agree that Malcolm's murderer was one Freddie Drayton, an English thug whose last known address was in Marbella.'

'You've seen the photograph of one of Freddie Drayton's previous victims,' said Sam pointing at the photograph Paul had copied for us on Paulo's desk. 'You can see his unique trademark, which he has so far according to the British police left on the necks of ten murder victims. It's exactly the same.'

'Also,' I chipped in, 'the people that did this, and we all agree it was Derek Clive Simpson and his gang, obviously knew that the stones were in Malcolm's safe at the villa, and therefore they must have had inside information from either London, Amsterdam or South Africa.'

'Wherever the information came from,' said Sam, 'you can be sure it wasn't passed on to a part time Romanian gardener named Alexandru. You have to release him, Paulo, before the newspapers make the GNR look foolish yet again.'

'I agree with you both, and at this stage I'm prepared to release Alexandru on police bail provided we keep his passport, which we already have, and that he checks in with me here every day. I can't just let him walk away and flee back to Romania, even though I think that is highly unlikely.'

'Thank you, Paulo,' said Sam, 'you are a very fair man.'

'What will you two do next, or are you happy to leave it to us now?'

'No disrespect, Paulo, but there are things we can do that you can't, such as flying to South Africa to see if we can find where the information came from, or perhaps search for the gang in Spain.'

'Well I wish you luck, and as I requested before—please, both of you—be safe and keep me informed.'

We bid Paulo farewell with the assurance that Alexandru would be back home with his family by the end of the day. We both went back to my villa at Quinta do Lago via Andrei and Cristina's house and brought them up to date about Alexandru's imminent return. Once back at the villa, we had a lazy evening curled up on the sofa watching various American crime programmes on Sky TV.

Chapter Nine

We chatted at length about what our next move should be, and came to the conclusion that we had to find where the leak came from, and who they'd passed the information on to, although we were fairly confident we already knew who had received it. We felt that we needed those answers before we could tackle anything else. We looked at several options, and talked around the subject for nearly two hours, but in the end decided that we had no choice but to go to South Africa if we wanted answers. Neither of us had ever been there before, but Jeremy Green, the Manager at Malcolm's Hatton Garden jewellery shop, had mentioned the name of the courier and his company. That had to be our starting point. Sam suggested telephoning him at the shop to see if he, hopefully now having had a good night's sleep, could help us with any more information.

Sam telephoned Mr Green, who she soon discovered was actually very friendly having got over the shock of Malcolm's death, and he insisted Sam call him Jeremy. He was also extremely helpful in answering as many of Sam's questions as he could. Apparently, all the stolen stones had come from De Beers's flagship "Venetia" diamond mine in Limpopo Province which had opened in 1992. Jeremy told Sam that he'd actually visited the mine twice with Malcolm—once in

2005, and again three years ago. Jeremy Green also told us that it was not the easiest place in the world to get to, and involved a long flight to Pretoria, and then a shorter internal flight to what is now called Polokwane, but was previously called Pietersburg before the ANC changed a lot of town names. Reaching the mine is then a lengthy cross country drive of several hours over pretty rugged countryside. What fun!

To be honest, we were both undecided about heading off to South Africa. The other alternative was to head to Marbella and see if we could find Derek and his compatriots. Then it hit suddenly me.

'Sam,' I said. 'Forget about South Africa for the moment—why don't we go to Spain and try and employ Mr Dominic St Clair, Derek's tame lawyer, on some pretext or other. I assume he still needs to earn a living, and he probably advertises his services somewhere. If we find him and then secretly follow him, he's bound to lead us to Derek, Freddie and co.'

'Mmm,' replied an unconvinced Sam. 'We could easily drive to Marbella, no problem, but as soon as we get there and start asking questions about St Clair, we could be the next two people with pinking sheared throats. We need to think out our next move very carefully.'

We did just that, and in the end took a few days to go through our options. We didn't want to rush into anything and end up getting ourselves in trouble.

'I suppose the first question we have to ask ourselves,' I started, 'is, why we are continuing to get involved in all this. Alexandru, who as you pointed out we don't actually know is now back home with his family, albeit on bail, and you could say we've done our bit.'

'Yes, we may not know Alexandru,' replied Sam, 'but as you said, you certainly knew Malcolm, and I just feel that having gone this far we really need to see it through. I know it's a bit risky, but if we take our time and are careful, I'm sure we'll be fine.'

I was about to respond when my mobile rang.

'Ah, good morning, Mr Turner, it's Jeremy Green from Hatton Garden.'

'Good morning to you too, Jeremy, and how are you?' I asked, not really having a clue what he wanted or why he was telephoning me.

'I'm fine thank you, in fact I'm feeling rather good at the moment. If you recall, you asked me a few days ago when you were in the shop who would benefit from Malcolm's death in the sense of who would get the business. Well I've just had a telephone call from the solicitor for Miss Caroline Chambers who was Malcolm's only god daughter. Not being married or having any children of his own, it seems Malcolm left ninety percent of the business to his god daughter, and very surprisingly, I have been left the other ten percent. Miss Chamber's solicitor telephoned me and said I would receive a share certificate for my part of the business in due course, and that he and Miss Chambers would call at the shop this coming Wednesday to discuss the future of the business.'

'Well congratulations, Jeremy,' I said. 'Tell me if you don't mind me asking, I assume you've met her—what is Miss Chambers like?'

'Well I can't say I know her very well, I've only met her three times. I guess she must be about thirty years old, brunette, fairly tall, quite thin and she wears gold rim glasses.'

'Thanks for that, but I meant her persona rather than her build and looks.'

'Oh, I see. Well, all I can say is that she is the opposite of Malcolm. Mr Tisbury was always very polite to me, was always extremely punctual, and he was kind to everybody. Miss Chambers always comes across to me as being quite rude and always wanting her own way. I suggested a time next Wednesday morning for the meeting, but she said I'd have to change it to the afternoon as her solicitor has to fly in for the meeting. She didn't ask, she just insisted.'

'Sorry Jeremy, you say her solicitor had to fly in—do you, by any chance, know where he's coming from and what his name is?'

'Yes I do as it happens, I wrote if down. He is flying to Gatwick from Malaga, and I clearly remember his name as it's quite distinctive. It's Mr Dominic St Clair.

After I'd thanked Jeremy for the information and put the phone down I relayed everything I had just heard to Sam. Needless to say, hearing that Dominic St Clair was Caroline Chambers's solicitor set off alarm bells for us both.

'It can't just be a coincidence, can it?' asked Sam

'Well I suppose it could be,' I replied, 'but I think the chances of the gang we are sure committed the theft and the murder having the same solicitor as the inheritor of Malcolm's estate is a million to one chance of being a coincidence. No, she's linked to this somehow.'

'I don't think we have a choice now,' said Sam, 'we have to head for Marbella and do a bit of snooping.'

'I agree. Now listen, Sam, I've got a vague idea, but I think it makes sense. If Dominic St Clair is having his meeting with Jeremy on Wednesday afternoon, he'll be flying back either on a late flight Wednesday night or first thing Thursday morning. If we can be at Malaga airport and watch the passengers from the late flight disembark, we'll either see him as he comes through, and if he's not on that flight we can simply go back to our hotel for the night. The following day however, we can go back in time for the morning flight from Gatwick, then assuming he's on it, we can then follow him. We could be well on the way to finding where Derek and his gang are all based.

'So do we get a flight to Malaga from Faro and then hire a car,' suggested Sam, 'or do we just drive there using one of our own cars. It's only about four hours?'

'Well as much as I hate saying this,' I began, 'why don't we drive there in your car. We stand less chance of being spotted as it doesn't stand out as much as mine, and we'll also have our own transport ready to go wherever and whenever we need it.'

'Sounds like a plan, when do think we should leave?' asked Sam.

'Tuesday morning should be fine. That'll get us there in plenty of time to find a decent hotel near the airport, and check out the various flight options to and from Gatwick. We can be at the airport on Wednesday morning, and with any luck we might see him catch the flight to Gatwick. Then we should know which airline he's flying with, and later hopefully the possible times of his return flight.'

'So we've got a couple of days before we leave,' said Sam. 'How long should we pack for, do you think? Just a few days or longer?'

'I guess the trouble is we have no idea what we're going to find. I think we need to be very careful throughout this trip Sam, because if anything goes wrong we can't call on Inspector Cabrita for back up as we'll be in a different country. We'll be very much on our own. As for clothes, well I think to be on the safe side we should take enough for a week, and if necessary we can always buy some more underwear and socks, or failing that I could just send you off to the local laundromat while I watch football on the TV.'

'On your bike, Turner,' laughed Sam. 'I may love you, but I definitely draw the line at washing your smelly pants and socks. At least until we're married.'

'Oh, so you think we'll be getting married sometime do you?' I asked with a smile.

'It depends,' Sam retorted, 'I haven't quite worked out yet if you're husband material or not. You'll just have to keep working on trying to impress me.'

'I don't know,' I smiled back, 'you just can't get decent staff these days.'

It was at that point that Sam threw another paperback at me.

Chapter Ten

We set off bright and early on Tuesday morning. If you live in the Algarve and you decide to drive to anywhere in Spain, you always have to bear in mind that you will have to go via Seville. Not that there is anything wrong with Seville, it is in fact a lovely city with some wonderful sights, it's simply that because it is the only route to get anywhere, it is always busy and Tuesday morning was no exception. Firstly you get on to, and then drive west to east along the A22 in the Algarve, which is more or less a two lane motorway, and you eventually cross the Guadiana River, which is also the border between Portugal and Spain. The A22 becomes the A49 as soon as you get into Spain and you simply stay on this road passing Huelva until you get to the outskirts of Seville. At Seville you have a choice. You can keep going straight and follow the A92 as it eventually takes you to southern Spain through Antequera, Málaga, Benalmadena, Fuengirola and then Marbella. The other option and the one we chose was to turn right as soon as you hit Seville, and then take the E5 due south heading for Gibraltar. Once you see the famous rock in front of you, turn on to the E15 which leads you into Marbella and eventually Málaga.

We arrived at the airport around 2:00 pm having taken a leisurely drive. We left Sam's car in the short term car park and headed into the terminal. We checked the departures board to see which airlines flew to London Gatwick. There were four airlines offering daily flights: Norwegian Air International, British Airways, EasyJet, and Spain's own airline Iberia. Sam hit on the idea of pretending to be Mrs St Clair, and she then went from check-in desk to check-in desk, apologising for disturbing them, smiling nicely at the staff and asking if they could possibly help her. She spun the line that her husband was booked onto a flight to Gatwick tomorrow, but she had no idea with which airline. His mobile phone seemed to be dead, and so he was out of touch at the moment, and tomorrow he would simply be passing through the airport from an incoming flight from Malta, and she needed to meet him with some papers he needed for his meeting later that day in London. She had no luck with British Airways or Iberia, but she eventually found the name Dominic St Clair booked onto the ten past ten morning flight with EasyJet.

We left the airport and checked into our hotel for the rest of the day, the rather splendid "Vincci Selección Aleysa Hotel Boutique & Spa". It was a five star beach front hotel about five miles out of Malaga heading towards Benalmadena. It was quite expensive, but it was certainly worth it. We had a wonderful large room with a massive balcony overlooking the sea, and the hotel's public areas were fantastically clean and modern. Everything was all cream coloured, from floor tiles to leather sofas. We'd brought our swimming things with us, so we got changed and spent the next few hours relaxing round the pool and drinking the occasional ice cold beer. After a very relaxing afternoon, we drove into Marbella and found a restaurant serving really good Brazilian steak, which we washed down with a bottle of Merlot, our favourite red wine.

The following morning, we got to the airport in time to watch Dominic St Clair board his flight to Gatwick and then spent the rest of the morning watching the idle rich lounging on their yachts in Puerto Banus Marina. If you don't know it and have never been there, Puerto Banus is a very fashionable marina full of multi-million pound yachts just outside Marbella and is "the place to be seen". We had hoped we might catch a glimpse of Derek Simpson as he seemed the sort of flash sod that would possibly buy a yacht, or even rent one, but no such luck. So after a light lunch we drove back to our hotel and repeated yesterday's adventures by the pool before returning to the same restaurant in the evening where Sam had a pepper steak and I, being very boring, had some more of their wonderful Brazilian steak and Merlot. Dominic St Clair was scheduled to arrive back in Málaga on EasyJet's nineteen-twenty flight from London Gatwick arriving at Málaga just after 11pm. That suited us fine because that late at night there was only one place he could be going. Home.

Sure enough, Dominic arrived on the flight as expected and he came straight through as he had no hold bags, only his hand luggage. Sam had been sitting in her Merc in the drop off area at the car park with the engine running, and as soon as I emerged, she pulled up to collect me as Dominic climbed into the back of a taxi and drove out of the airport. It was a pitch black night and we knew that even if Dominic looked back all he would see was a pair of headlights in the distance. You couldn't tell one car from another at that time of night. We followed from a safe distance as his taxi sped along the AP7 heading towards Marbella, but then just as it approached La Capellania, the taxi turned off the main road and onto the smaller A368 heading north. We knew there was only one town on that road—Mijas. The taxi headed into the small town, turned two or three times while we carefully kept our distance. Then the taxi deposited Dominic outside the gates of a beautiful large white villa. He paid the taxi which then drove off, looked both up and down the road and then went into the villa. We had already parked up and turned both our lights and the engine off about a hundred yards behind them when his taxi had stopped, and there was no way he'd know he'd been followed. After Dominic had gone inside, we waited about ten minutes, and then drove slowly past the villa noting the name, before heading back to our hotel. Upon our return we asked the hotel receptionist if she had any information on a small town up in the hills above Marbella named Mijas. We were absolutely amazed when she handed us about fifteen different leaflets and pamphlets.

We returned to our room and started reading about Mijas. The leaflets told us that is a typical Andalusian white-washed village, located on a mountainside about 430 metres or 1,476 feet above sea level, in the heart of the Costa del Sol region. Apparently the economy of Mijas is based mainly on tourism, and there are thousands of visitors in the town every week. When the receptionist gave us the leaflets, she also told us lots of information we wouldn't find in any leaflets. She told us that dotted all around Mijas are literally hundreds of private villas and small estates tucked into the hills. She also said that most of them were surrounded by high walls and high hedges, and most of the villas also have very thick high wooden gates. She also said she didn't know for sure, but she estimated at least ninety percent of them also had CCTV cameras on permanent watch. After a couple of cups of tea in our room we decided to become tourists the following day and pay our own visit to the little white town in the hills.

I have to say we both loved the feel of Mijas the minute we got there. It looked and felt totally different from our nocturnal visit the night before. The lower part of town where you first arrive and park your car, was absolutely chock-a-block with tourist shops selling all the usual cheap tat from sombreros, leather goods and stuffed donkeys to little girls bright red and black flamenco dresses and the usual selection of tee shirts and polo shirts. However, once you got to the higher parts of Mijas, it all changed. It had numerous wonderful cobbled streets, all with fantastic shops where you could buy anything you want; from really expensive jewellery to big brand watches, designer handbags, designer shoes etc. There was also what felt like hundreds of bars and restaurants, and because of its location high in the hills, most of them had amazing views out to sea. We kept walking uphill and eventually we passed the old bull ring, which is now a small museum and no longer hosts fights. Then we reached a large open area with lovely gardens where you can look out to sea and also look down on the hundreds of private villas built into the hills. My gut instinct told me that Derek and Sandra Simpson were down there somewhere in one of the up-market villas—but how the hell were we going to find out which one?

The white village of Mijas, near Marbella, Costa del Sol, southern Spain

The some of the 80 restaurants, cafes and bars of Mijas

One of the many small squares in Mijas

The scenic viewing gardens near the bullring in Mijas

Chapter Eleven

Having got back to our hotel around lunchtime, we sat in two extremely comfortable leather armchairs in the bar with a bottle of our favourite Merlot, a couple of toasted cheese and ham sandwiches and a bowl of chips. We chatted through what we now knew making notes as we went, and then tried to think of ways of discovering what we didn't know.

'Firstly,' I began, 'we know, although we have no proof, that Malcolm was murdered by Freddie Drayton. His unique way of cutting throats gives the game away.'

'If Freddie Drayton is the murderer,' said Sam, 'and we know he works exclusively for Derek Simpson, then we are ninety-nine percent sure Derek Simpson was the brains behind the robbery of the two and a half million pounds worth of uncut diamonds missing from Malcolm's safe.'

'Yes, but yet again we have no proof,' I added.

'We're pretty sure that Dominic St Clair is the link between Derek Simpson and Caroline Chambers,' said Sam, 'but we have no idea how to prove it.'

'And the leaked information must have come from either Jeremy Green or Pieter Van Straaten, the courier for De Beers,' I surmised. 'They were the only two people apart from Malcolm himself who knew when the stones would be in his safe.'

'I'm afraid my old police colleagues,' began Sam, 'would all say the same thing. This is all nothing but conjecture on our part, and with not an ounce of evidence or concrete proof to be seen anywhere. We need to start getting some proof.'

'I agree,' I replied. 'My thoughts for what they are worth is that we are now left with no choice. We have to find out who the leak was, and that means a visit to South Africa. I don't think we have any choice if we're going to make any progress in this case.'

'In this case eh?' joked Sam. 'Aren't we sounding like a professional investigator?'

'Yes, well I'm afraid it's really getting to me now. My friend Malcolm, admittedly not that close a friend, but nevertheless a friend, has been brutally murdered and we are sure we know who did it. I'm also fairly sure there is evidence to be found in South Africa, but neither the British or Portuguese police are going to visit there, so I guess that leaves us?'

'Well I think we've done all we can here for the time being,' said Sam. 'We now know where Dominic St Clair lives, but short of knocking on his front door and asking him for Derek Simpson's address, I'm not sure what else we can do or what progress we can make.'

'No, you're right, we're done here for the time being. I guess we could try and follow Dominic in the hope he'd lead us to the Simpsons, but we're not professionals spooks, and I'm pretty sure we'd soon be spotted and then we'd find Freddie Drayton coming after us.'

'OK then,' said Sam. 'Let's get our things together, pay the bill, which you're paying by the way, and then head back to the Algarve and organise some flights to South Africa.'

'I presume I'm paying for those as well?' I asked.

‘As you said,’ replied Sam. ‘Malcolm was your friend. No, in all seriousness, I’ll pay for my own flights, and now we are a proper couple we ought to share everything, including the cost of solving “our case” as you call it.’

We did as Sam had suggested and arrived back at my villa in the early evening. I booked two one-way tickets to South Africa as we had no idea how long we would need to be there. It was going to be a long journey. Firstly, we had to get to the UK as flying anywhere from Faro usually meant having to go to London first. So the following day we boarded the lunch time British Airways flight from Faro to London Gatwick, and then got a bus link round to London Heathrow where we grabbed a bite to eat before boarding the nine thirty-five flight to Cape Town. We’d decided to eat at the airport as I’d booked business seats for us. It was an overnight flight on a Seven Four Seven and that meant we could lie flat and get a good night’s sleep ignoring the meal service. We arrived in Cape Town at eleven in the morning local time and had four hours to kill before boarding the four o’clock local flight to Pretoria with SA Airlink. We eventually arrived in Pretoria at six-fifteen in the evening absolutely knackered. We got a taxi to our hotel, the Sheraton in Stanza Bopape Street, checked in and then grabbed a quick meal in the restaurant before turning in for the night.

The following morning, we felt much better having had a good night’s sleep. We decided to go for a swim in the hotel pool before having a decent breakfast, after which we returned to our room to plan what we were doing next.

‘Well firstly, I guess there’s no rush,’ I said, ‘so let’s take our time and be as professional as we can in how we go about finding answers to the many questions we’ve have. We don’t want to tip anyone off about what we're up to, or get ourselves into hot water.'

'Agreed,' responded Sam, 'so let's write down the questions we need answers to, and work out a few ideas on how we go about getting those answers.' I always carried a little black notebook with me everywhere I went. Most writers do as you never know when or where you're going to get the next great idea, and it's always good to have a means of making notes immediately. The notebooks I use are about five and a half inches by three and a half inches, have an elasticated band the holds the book shut, and a small elasticated loop on the side for hooking a pen into. Actually I never use a pen ever since I discovered Koh-I-Noor propelling pencils a few years ago. They are brilliant, having a strong black metal tube, a really thick pencil lead inside them and a sharpener built into the end. Anyway, I digress.

'I guess the first question,' began Sam, 'is how do we find Pieter Van Straaten and how do we arrange a meeting with him?'

'I may be wrong,' I said, 'but I don't think De Beers are involved in this in any way shape or form. They are the world's biggest diamond dealers, and while two a half million pounds worth of diamonds seems a lot of money to most people, to De Beers it will be less than small change. They just couldn't be bothered.'

'I agree,' replied Sam, 'so are you suggesting we just go to De Beers, tell them about the robbery and the murder and ask them to help?'

'No, I don't think I am. I'm simply ruling them out at this stage. If this was a plot for one of my crime novels, you and I would dream up some device like having got a rich uncle who's died and left us 50 million pounds in his will, provided we do something with it and not just blow it. We could say we've talked about it and we like the idea of opening an upmarket jewellers in Hatton Garden selling diamond and white gold pieces, and we wanted to know if De Beers would supply us with the stones. Also, can they recommend one or two good stone cutters and how do we go about setting everything up. We could include a question about how the stones would get to us, and are the transport people trustworthy carrying such high value merchandise or something like that.'

'That sounds brilliant to me,' said Sam. 'Did you just make all that up as you went along or had you already thought it out?'

'No, I just started talking and made it up. I guess having been a writer for most of my adult life, my brain now just seems to work like that. One thing though, I don't think we should use our real names and I also think it will sound better and look better to De Beers if we tell them we're a married couple. Before you say anything sarcastic,' I smiled, 'and start making out I'm proposing, I'm not. This is just for De Beers benefit, but rest assured young lady, I'm pretty sure the time will come, but in the meantime, don't get ahead of yourself!'

'As if?' laughed Sam.

We adopted the basic idea and in theory became Mr and Mrs Michael and Samantha Peters. We'd decided to use our own Christian names in case we accidentally slipped up during conversation, and we then went into Pretoria's main high street and called in at a jewellers where we bought a costume jewellery wedding and engagement ring set. We knew it wouldn't convince anyone from De Beers that they were the real thing, but we'd decided we'd bring the subject up ourselves and would simply say our real rings were locked in our safe back in London, as we didn't want to tempt fate and have them stolen in a country we didn't really know.

I telephoned De Beers head office in Johannesburg and asked if there was someone we could talk to in Pretoria about setting up a new business in conjunction with De Beers. I was put through to a Mr Marius Van der Byl, who introduced himself as De Beers's New Business Director. He informed me that unfortunately there was nobody in Pretoria that we could talk to as it was simply a production area for the Venetia mine only. However he said if we could possibly be in Johannesburg tomorrow, then he would be delighted to meet with us and talk through our ideas over lunch, as his guests. I accepted the invitation and then told Sam we were on the move again. We quickly checked out of the Sheraton, got a taxi to Polokwane airport and caught the next flight to Johannesburg. An hour later we touched down, hired a small Renault Clio from Avis, and then went straight to the Westcliff hotel where I had booked us in for a couple of nights, with an option to extend should we need longer.

The following day we met up with Marius Van der Byl in his very plush office on the corner of Crownwood Road and Diamond Drive in the heart of Johannesburg.

'It's very kind of you to meet with us at such short notice Mr Van der Byl,' I began.

'Please, call me Marius,' he interrupted. 'The trouble with South African names is they are usually several syllables, and quite often several words in length. I find if you don't want to double the length of conversations it's much easier just to use first names only. Do you mind if I call you Michael and Samantha?'

'Not at all, and if you don't mind I much prefer Sam,' responded my new pretend wife. 'It always seems so much friendlier to me.'

'Excellent,' responded Marius. 'Michael and Sam it is then. Now on the telephone you said you had been left a large sum of money and were hoping to go into business, possibly getting involved with ourselves. Could you explain more and let me see if there is something we can do together.'

'Well,' I began, 'our late uncle Charles died recently.' Sam then interrupted as we'd rehearsed back at the hotel.

'Yes, it was from throat cancer, very sad really as he was only sixty two years old, but he wouldn't give up the cigarettes despite all the warnings he'd had.'

'Anyway,' I continued, 'Uncle Charles left us roughly 50 million pounds in his will.'

'He was in oil you know!' interrupted Sam again. We'd decided Sam would constantly interrupt in the early stages so that Marius couldn't concentrate too hard on the story I was spinning him, and see any holes in it. We didn't think there were any holes, but it was better to be safe than sorry.

'The money was left to us with Uncle Charles's one stipulation that we did something business-like with it,' I said, 'and not just squander it on fast cars and yachts.'

'I don't really like yachts anyway,' said Sam. 'I'm not a very good swimmer. But one thing I do love is really good jewellery and I know top quality when I see it. So I thought about setting up a high end jewellery business in Hatton Garden. We live in Central London and so we can walk to Hatton Garden. It would be so convenient.'

'I quite liked the idea as I've yet to meet a poor jeweller,' I said while smiling, 'and I'd heard of De Beers as being the only company to get involved with if you wanted to trade in diamonds. We thought we'd concentrate on really top end pieces in white gold and diamonds.'

'An excellent choice if I might say,' responded Marius.

'Would De Beers be interested in supplying us with the stones?' I asked. 'I know fifty million is not large by De Beers's standards, but our aim would be to see it grow considerably over the years.'

'Oh let me assure you Michael, fifty million pounds, and I assume we are talking sterling here, is a lot of money to anyone or any company, even one as large as De Beers. And yes of course we would be absolutely delighted to supply you with whatever stones you may want. How soon do you envisage starting?'

'Well as soon as we get back to London,' I said, 'we hope to acquire an existing jewellery shop in Hatton Garden. We've seen a property we quite like, and our solicitor is currently looking at acquiring it for us on a ten year lease. We didn't want to buy as we want the flexibility of being able to move should we need to.'

'Mmm. Very sensible,' mused Marius.

'We've also tentatively got ourselves an experienced manager for the shop from a rival Hatton Garden jeweller,' said Sam. 'He'll be joining us as soon as we're set up and ready to go. We both felt we needed someone who knows the business inside out, and can offer us help and guidance in the early stages.'

'Again, that sounds eminently sensible,' mused Marius, 'you've obviously both got your heads screwed on if you'll pardon the expression.'

'Of course,' chipped in Sam.

Now came the tricky part in how to ask the questions we really needed answers to without giving the game away.

‘Excuse my ignorance, Marius,’ I began, ‘but could you tell us a little bit about De Beers and how it works, and could you also possibly recommend one or two good stone cutters?’

‘Can I also ask you something that’s worrying me,’ asked Sam. ‘I must be honest, the thought of all those stones travelling from South Africa to London worries the life out of me. Tell me—do they ever get stolen?’

Marius started laughing and dismissed Sam’s question straight away.

‘Excuse me for laughing, Sam,’ said Marius, ‘I assure you I’m not laughing at you, but at the terrible prospect of us not having complete confidence in getting the product to the customer. I can tell you straight—we would have gone out of business over a hundred years ago if that was a problem. Let me fill you in a little bit on De Beers.’

‘De Beers is a massive world-wide company with just two shareholders. They are Anglo–American, who own eighty-five per cent and the Government of the Republic of Botswana who own the other fifteen per cent. As a company we’re involved in almost every stage of the diamond pipeline: exploration, mining, sorting, valuing and selling rough diamonds. We also market and sell polished diamonds and jewellery, and lastly we are developing synthetic diamonds for industrial use. As I said, De Beers is a massive world-wide company which currently employs more than 20,000 people around the world. The parent company is De Beers Société Anonyme, which was incorporated in 2000 in Luxembourg, and that is where our head office is located and where the Board of Directors meets. Our commercial activities are carried out in numerous different parts of the world by a whole range of subsidiaries, investments and joint ventures, but they are all part of De Beers. The company pays its taxes and royalties to the respective governments in the countries and jurisdictions where they operate.'

'I had no idea it was such a massive organisation,' I said although actually I did.

'In answer to your question about theft, Sam,' continued Marius. 'To be perfectly honest, with diamonds being as small as they are and at the same time as valuable as they are, we recognise that dealing with the risk of theft is an important part of our business. De Beers is governed by a risk framework through which risks in every area of the business are identified and managed. Each of our business units highlights any and all significant risks they can think of to the Board, which has devised a policy and strategy for dealing with all of them. Basically our approach is to reduce risk where we can't remove it entirely.'

'Sorry if I'm appearing thick, Marius,' said Sam, 'but how do you get the stones from here in South Africa to us in London, I assume they're not just posted, and if they are stolen, who pays?'

'OK. Firstly we have our own team of excellent couriers, and they personally carry the stones from us direct to the purchasing client. The stones are at all times kept in a locked case which is handcuffed to the courier's wrist, and the carrying courier always has a second courier with him riding shotgun at all times until delivery has taken place and the stones have been signed for. The second courier is always licensed to carry a firearm at all times, and we have agreements allowing us to carry firearms with every airline we use, and all the relevant police forces in the countries we deal with. As for who pays if anything should happen such as theft, then De Beers has very hefty insurance coverage. Your money is in no danger until you have taken delivery of the stones, checked them and signed to that effect.

'Wow,' Sam replied. 'That's impressive. Tell me Marius, do your couriers stay with you long. I'd have thought you must have a very high turnover of courier staff as it seems a very risky and dangerous profession to be involved in.'

'Oh no, not at all, Sam. We have several couriers who have been with us well over twenty years. In fact I'm sorry to say two of our most experienced couriers are now coming up to retirement age. We retire all staff at sixty five, but they all receive a very generous pension from the company. One of them, Pieter Van Straaten has been with De Beers for over thirty three years and Pieter sadly retires next week. The other courier, Jan Joubert has been with us twenty eight years and he retires next month. Jan has recently got divorced and decided he wants to spend more time with the real love of his life—deep sea fishing.'

Without realising it, Marius Van der Byl had answered one of our un-asked questions. Pieter Van Straaten was retiring next week, and my immediate thought, and I'm pretty sure Sam will have thought the same, was that his cut from the theft of Malcolm's stones would make an extremely healthy contribution to his retirement fund. But then I had a nasty thought. That was only if the Simpsons let him live long enough to enjoy it.

We had an excellent lunch with Marius at the Inanda Polo Club Terrace Restaurant in Forest Road, of which Marius was a long standing member, although he didn't actually play himself. Marius described it as one of the clubs in Johannesburg you simply had to belong to if you wanted to meet the right kind of potential clients for De Beers new business, and I guess we were now in that category. We enjoyed a couple of bottles of Grangehurst 2006, which Marius informed us was a Bordeaux blend of Cabernet Sauvignon, Merlot and Petit Verdot and was the flagship wine of one of the best estates in South Africa. Between the three of us, we sank two bottles with our lunch, followed by a round of very fine ports. Then we bid farewell to Marius promising him that our solicitor would be in touch, and we then made our way back to our hotel. The next task was to try and have a little chat with Pieter Van Straaten, and would you believe it—he was listed in the Johannesburg telephone directory.

Cape Town from the Gulfstream

Typical diamond necklace and pendant

Polished diamonds before mounting and setting

One of De Beers diamond mines in South Africa

Chapter Twelve

I decided not to telephone Pieter Van Straaten, but to simply arrive at his front door. The telephone directory told us that he lived in Parnell Road, just across the main road near Cruywagen Park. We left the hotel around 9:00 am, found Parnell Road and knocked on his front door just before 9:30 am. The door was answered by a man who I guessed was Pieter Van Straaten as the man appeared to be in his sixties.

'Mr Pieter Van Straaten?' I asked.

'Yes, that's me,' he said. 'How can I help you?'

'Good morning, Mr Van Straaten. I'm not sure if you are aware of this, but the two and half million pounds worth of uncut diamonds you helped to steal in the Algarve led directly to the murder of their owner Mr Malcolm Tisbury.'

'Oh my God,' said Van Straaten and all the colour drained from his face.

'Are you the police?' he asked.

'No,' I replied. 'We're private investigators from Portugal working in conjunction with both the Portuguese police and the British police. The murdered man was British. Can we come in please, and if you willingly help us with our enquiries we may be able to keep your involvement out of this. Are you alone in the house?'

'Yes,' replied Van Straaten. 'I live alone. My wife sadly died three years ago.'

We entered the house and he took us into the lounge where the three of us sat down.

'Look, we aren't interested in you particularly, and if you co-operate and answer all our questions, we'll forget we ever met you. We want the murderer, not the small fry.'

'Yes, that's me—small fry,' said Van Straaten.

'OK. Fill me in. How did you get involved and give me names and dates where you can.' I passed my notebook and pencil to Sam as I spoke. 'My colleague here will take notes as we speak, and please remember—this is your one and only chance Van Straaten, so don't mess us about.'

I suddenly felt like Sam Spade or Sherlock Holmes, but Van Straaten didn't know that.

'I got a telephone call from a British lawyer about three weeks ago, I can't remember his name exactly but I think it was Dominic something or other.'

'St Clair?' I offered.

'Yes, that was it—Dominic St Clair. He said he had an offer for me which would make my life in retirement a lot easier, and all I had to do was give him some information.'

'What did he ask for? I enquired.

'Well I wasn't interested at first. Diamond couriers frequently get propositioned by various crooks and thieves once people know what you do for a living, it's all part of the job, and De Beers even train you in how to respond to various different approaches, plus there's a helpline for you to report all approaches.'

'I assume you never reported the phone call?'

'Well no, I was going to, but St Clair said nobody would get hurt, it was going to be a completely victimless crime unless you included the loss to the mega rich insurance company, and he said I'd be richer to the tune of one hundred thousand pounds sterling. That's an absolute fortune for me, that's roughly two million South African Rand. It was my opportunity to retire with some decent money, move to the coast and live the sort of life I'd always wanted.'

'So what did you have to do to earn your money?'

'He said he'd been told by a client of his that there was a customer of De Beers named Malcolm Tisbury who was due to receive a large parcel of uncut diamonds in the next two weeks or so. All I had to do was to make sure I got the courier job, and then telephone him to say when the delivery was being made, and then telephone him again once Mr Tisbury had signed for them. That was it.'

'How did you know you'd get paid? After all, this was obviously a bent lawyer and a bunch of crooks you were dealing with.'

'I asked for twenty percent up front to show good faith on their part. St Clair agreed and he wire transferred the money into my account the same day.'

'How did you ensure you were the courier?'

'Oh that was relatively easy. I told Francois Viljoen, he's my boss and the man in charge of all the couriers that I had got a very sick cousin in Portugal, and if a job came up anywhere in Portugal could I please have it, and then after I'd made the delivery I could take a few days off to visit my sick cousin, as it may be the last opportunity I got to see him.'

'I presume he took the bait and you got the job?'

'Yes. I phoned St Clair and gave him the delivery dates, and confirmed that I would telephone him once the delivery had been made. In fairness he transferred the balance of eighty thousand pounds as soon as I'd confirmed I'd made the delivery, and I've never heard from him since. I promise you, I had no idea violence was going to be used or that anyone was going to get killed.'

'I believe you. You mentioned earlier that St Clair had said he'd been told there was a client of De Beers named Malcolm Tisbury due to receive a parcel of uncut stones. Did St Clair tell you how he knew that, or the name of the person that told him?'

'No, he never mentioned her name.'

'Her name you just said—so St Clair's client was a woman?'

'Yes, didn't I say that? Sorry. Honestly, I know no more than what I've told you. Please believe me, I wouldn't have got involved if I'd thought for one minute that anyone was going to get hurt, let alone murdered.'

'Look, Van Straaten. You obviously don't know the people you've got yourself hooked up with, but I tell you now—they're nasty, extremely dangerous and vicious, and they don't like leaving loose ends. As far as they will be concerned—you are definitely a loose end.

I suggest you pack up all your worldly goods today, change your name and move to somewhere nobody's ever heard of you, because if you don't, I think you'll find yourself with a newly sliced and diced throat. I suggest you leave Johannesburg, and if you want to stay alive do it straight away. I don't condone for one minute what you've done, but I won't be saying anything to the authorities. It won't bring back to life the murdered victim, and I do believe you would have had no part in it had you known. Goodbye Van Straaten—I hope we never meet again.' I got up, and Sam and I left the house.

'Wow. Very Inspector Morse I thought, maybe with a hint of Bergerac, and possibly with a slight touch of the Sweeney's

Jack Regan swagger thrown in for good measure,' said Sam. 'You were brilliant, Mr Peters, and I must say I enjoyed playing Doctor Watson to your Sherlock Holmes.'

'Aren't we overdoing the detective similarities just a bit—Sherlock Holmes, Inspector Morse, Bergerac, Jack Regan. To be honest my main concern was that I was about to turn into Inspector Clouseau at any minute.'

Sam and I laughed as we climbed into our small hire car and headed back to our hotel. We went straight up to our room, reviewed what we'd learnt from our two meetings while they were fresh in our minds, making copious notes as we did so. We eventually came to the conclusion that it had been a very useful trip, but there was nothing else to be found out at this stage by staying any longer in South Africa. So we booked our return flights and were back at my villa in the Algarve two days later.

Chapter Thirteen

Sam seemed to have more or less moved in with me, and not that I'm complaining, but we'd only spent one night apart since we first shared our real feelings with each other.

'Do you need me to empty a few drawers in the bedroom, and make some space in one of the wardrobes?' I asked.

'Why do I only get one of the wardrobes?' Sam asked, and then started laughing.

'Yes please,' she said, 'that would be really great. I don't intend to move in—well at least not yet, but it would be nice to have somewhere to keep a few clothes rather than having to drive home to Loulé every time I need some clean knickers or a clean dress.'

Loulé was a town up in the hills beyond Almancil and it was where Sam had bought a house when she first moved to the Algarve. Unlike me, Sam had actually purchased a property rather than rented one, and she still loved her house which was very traditional Portuguese in style, but with a new modern extension at the back which had a wonderful view to the coast.

'I need to spend a few days at work,' exclaimed Sam, 'before my patients all leave me and sign up with another doctor. I don't think there's a great deal more we can do until we have found Caroline Chambers, who at this stage we know nothing about. Can I leave that with you while I go and organise my appointments with Jan?'

'Of course,' I replied, and with that Sam gave me a quick peck on the cheek, picked up her bag, left the villa and drove to her surgery. I assumed she would be gone for the rest of the day, and decided to make notes on everything we'd discovered on my laptop.

Sam was right—I needed to find out as much as I could about Caroline Chambers. Normally I guess, if you want to find out about someone who has been left money or property in a will, the starting point would be her lawyer, but I could hardly ring Dominic St Clair. So I started searching the internet, but it was if she never existed. I also tried searching all the various social media possibilities, Facebook, Twitter, LinkedIn, Pinterest, Instagram etc. Believe me, I tried them all but found no mention of Caroline Chambers anywhere—at least, not the one we were after. So I decided to ring Jeremy Green, after all it was him that had mentioned her to us in the first place. I picked up the phone and started to dial his number at the shop, but then for some reason I couldn't put my finger on, I stopped and put the phone down.

I then realised that all I knew about Jeremy Green was what he had told me himself. I had no doubts that he was Malcolm's Shop Manager, but as for everything else, well I hadn't a clue if it was true or not. He could be telling me any old rubbish in the same way Sam and I had spun a believable yarn to Marius Van der Byl in Johannesburg. So I decided to try a different approach and I dialled Inspector Paul Naismith on the mobile number he'd given Sam and I when we'd visited him. It went straight to voicemail and I left him a message asking him to call me back as soon as he had five minutes to spare. About an hour later my mobile rang.

'Michael Turner,' I answered.

'Michael, hi. It's Paul Naismith. You rang me?'

'Paul, hi to you too and thanks for returning my call. Look, I wonder if you can help me.'

I then recounted to Paul what we'd learnt over the last few days, including our trip to South Africa and then I brought up my queries.

'I have to be honest, Paul, there are two people involved in this that I'm not sure about at all, and I wondered if you could find out a few details and possibly fill in some of the blanks. I'm sure they're both involved, but I'm not really sure how.'

'OK, give me names and addresses and I'll find out what I can and ring you back.'

'Ah, the problem is I only have their names, but I have no idea where they live.'

'Can you give me more than just names?' asked Paul.

'Well, Jeremy Green is the manager of Malcolm Tisbury's jewellery shop in Hatton Garden, and I assume you can trace him through that. As for Caroline Chambers, I know absolutely nothing about her other than she was left ninety percent of Malcolm's business in his will, but that I was told by Jeremy Green, and he was told I gather by her lawyer—who would you believe is the elusive Mr Dominic St Clair?'

'Oh excellent,' said Paul. 'I can hardly ask him. Leave it with me, I'll see what I can find out and come back to you. Oh, and well done you two in South Africa—you're turning into a right Hercule Poirot and Miss Marple aren't you. I'll get back to you as soon as I have any concrete news.'

'Thanks Paul,' I said and with that he switched off and ended the call from his end.

Paul telephoned me back about three hours later.

‘Well have I got some interesting news for you my friend,’ he began.

‘Hold on, Paul,’ I requested. ‘I want to make notes.’ I grabbed my notebook and pencil and switched my phone to speaker so that I didn’t have to hold it.

‘Right, fire away.’

‘Well in fact I’ve in fact got three addresses for you. The first is the house owned by Jeremy Green.’ Paul then gave me an address in New Cross, South London.

‘The second address is for Caroline Chambers and that is in the posh part of Islington?’

Paul then gave me that address as well.

‘You said you had three addresses for me. Whose is the third property?’

‘Well that’s the really interesting one, and I only came across this one when I did a purely exploratory search of names in an international directory. The third property is in the West Country—just outside Bath to be precise. It is a very large and secluded Georgian style country house set in nearly twenty acres of grounds, and it is currently worth about fifteen million pounds. It is officially the registered UK headquarters of “Thaxted Property Holdings”, an offshore property company based in the Bahamas. As well as the Bahamas headquarters, Thaxted also owns properties on several other Caribbean islands, Spain, Italy, Israel, Dubai, Oman and Brazil. As far as I can see from what records I could get my hands on, the company has an incredibly healthy bank balance and has no debts what so ever. When you dig a bit deeper that becomes quite an incredible achievement considering Thaxted Properties doesn’t actually trade with anyone, or as far as I can see sell anything at all. They don’t seem to do anything apart from buy multi-million pound properties around the world.'

'That's all very fascinating Paul, but how is it relevant to Malcolm's murder?'

'Now this is the really interesting bit. The property in Bath I mentioned just now and everything else owned by Thaxted Property Holdings is one hundred percent owned by the directors of the offshore company, who also happen to be the shareholders. I did some more digging, and it turns out that the Thaxted only has two directors.'

'Oh no, please don't tell me—Jeremy Green and Caroline Chambers.'

'Spot on, Michael. Look I don't know at this stage what's going on, but it looks to me as if Thaxted is an offshore company whose sole purpose in life is to launder money. Whatever Green and Chambers are up to you can be sure it's not legal. I'll keep looking my end, and please let me know if you come up with anything useful your end.'

'Thanks, Paul. I'll keep in touch. Bye'

'Cheers to you too, Hercule, and give my love to Miss Marple.'

I smiled as I put the phone down.

I was tempted to drive down to the surgery and fill Sam in on everything Paul had told me, but I decided not to disturb her first day back at work. However I didn't have to wait long as Sam got back around four o'clock. It was a lovely afternoon and I was itching to share the news with her, so I poured us both a glass of Merlot and we sat out by the pool.

'I have to tell you, Sam, I have had an incredibly productive day, thanks mainly to some amazing investigative work by Paul Naismith, who sends you his love by the way. Oh, you should know, after our Johannesburg investigations which I told him all about, he now calls me Hercule and you're Miss Marple.'

'That guy is crazy,' laughed Sam. 'But he's a great cop. So, what did Paul find out?'

I filled Sam in on my initial idea of ringing Jeremy for help as I couldn't find out anything about Caroline Chambers on the internet. I then told her how doubts had crept into my mind as I was in the process of telephoning him, and that thank goodness in the end I'd decided to ask Paul for help. Then, I told Sam everything Paul had discovered about the now mysterious Jeremy Green and the even more mysterious and secretive Caroline Chambers.

Sam was shocked to say the least as was I, and her first question had been running through my mind ever since I'd found out about the two directors of Thaxted Properties.

'If Jeremy Green is a director and fifty percent shareholder of a multi- million pound offshore company, what the hell is he doing working in a shop—albeit a very posh shop?'

'It has to be related to the movement of diamonds,' I guessed.

'But surely there are better ways of getting the information than working nine till five in a London store.'

'What if it is a way of laundering the stolen stones?'

'Well how would that work?' asked Sam.

'I'm obviously only guessing at this,' I said, 'but I've been thinking about that very thing ever since Paul told me. Jeremy and Caroline could for example be getting information on upcoming diamond shipments from various bent De Beers couriers we don't know about, and then be feeding that information to Derek Simpson through Dominic St Clair. Derek and the gang then arrange to steal the diamonds—and that could be from anywhere in the world, just as they did with Malcolm's. They probably have a deal of some sort with a good diamond cutter somewhere, and then Jeremy sells the stolen stones, now cut and polished and in some sort of fancy setting through the shop. Malcolm was in the Algarve most of the time and hardly ever around, and so he'd never know what was really going on. I'm guessing, but I would think the millions they make from the jewellery sales was then used to buy multi-million pound properties through Thaxted, the money therefore becoming laundered offshore and untraceable.'

'God, you are a clever sod aren't you,' said an admiring Sam.

'I'm probably totally wrong,' I replied, 'but even if I'm right that still doesn't get us any closer to Freddie Drayton, and he's the bastard I really want to see brought to justice.'

'I hate to say this, Michael, but I think we have to go back to Paul in Greenwich, lay it out just as you've done with me and see if we can put a plan together to bring all this crashing down round their heads, and in the process get Freddie Drayton.'

'You're right as usual. I'll go and start packing while you ring Jan and tell her you'll be away for another week or so.'

Chapter Fourteen

Inspector Paul Naismith had done a lot more digging by the time we arrived in Greenwich, and we went straight into a meeting with both Paul and Superintendent Stephen Colshaw in the Superintendent's very large office. We all sat in smart leather chairs at one end of a conference table that could seat ten people.

'What you two have stumbled on,' began Paul, 'now looks like becoming an absolutely massive case, possibly one of the biggest the world has seen involving vast fortunes in diamonds. As well as the British and Portuguese police, we now also have Interpol in South Africa and the Netherlands both involved.'

'We'll keep you both informed of course on progress,' said Superintendent Colshaw, 'and we have a few more questions for you both, but then you can leave it to us and head back to the Algarve sun.'

I wasn't just shocked at being dismissed, I was bloody annoyed.

'Piss off, Mr bloody Superintendent Sir,' I ranted getting up out of my chair.

'We brought you this case, we went to Spain and South Africa at our own expense and found out through our own skill and devices about the involvement of Dominic St Clair and the De Beers couriers. We gave you the names of Jeremy Green and Caroline Chambers and now you have the gall to tell us to butt out now there's a bit of glory in the offing. Well I'm sorry if it doesn't suit you Mr Superintendent, but my friend Malcolm Tisbury was brutally murdered and I intend to keep digging until his killer is brought to justice. If you don't like it arrest me, and I'll take you to the bloody court of human bloody rights in the Hague, and then I'll come back and slag you off on every TV show I can get on. The bloody nerve of you people.' I felt quite indignant at that point, and I'm not sure, but I think I'd let it show.

'I'm sorry, Paul,' said Sam standing up, 'and you too, Stephen, but Michael's right. Cutting us out at this stage is just not on, and to be honest I thought you were better than this. Come on Michael, let's leave them to it.'

'Oh for God's sake you two, sit down, shut up and listen to me!' exclaimed the Superintendent. 'Nobody is trying to cut you out, we're just trying to protect you as this looks like it could become not only massive, but also very nasty and bloody dangerous. If you want in, then that's fine by me, but we'll have to do it properly and we sign you both up as authorised police consultants. You will both have to sign the usual non-disclosure agreements, although Sam did that years ago when she became a police surgeon and it's probably still valid.'

'You might need to watch your temper a bit you know, Hercule!' smiled Paul.

'I'm sorry, you guys,' I replied, 'but it sounded for all the world as if you wanted Sam and me out, and I don't know if you noticed, but the thought of being excluded didn't make me very happy.'

'Did it—oh sorry, I never noticed,' smiled Paul.

‘No, not a thing,’ said a sniggering Stephen.

We both sat down again feeling better, and then Stephen picked up the phone and ordered a pot of tea and some biscuits. Stephen then opened a file on the desk, and Sam and I both signed forms to officially make us police consultants. Stephen had already prepared them while we were still on the plane, which proved to me he was being honest with us.

‘I have a theory for what it’s worth,’ I offered, ‘but I could easily be wrong on this.’

‘Go for it,’ said Stephen, and everyone took notes as I repeated my theory to the police.

‘You know that all makes an awful lot of sense,’ said Paul, ‘and if what you’ve outlined is the case, or something resembling it, then we’ll need numerous investigations undertaken all over the world, and done so without tipping those involved off.’

‘That’s why we’ve called in Interpol,’ said Stephen. ‘Two case officers have been appointed already, one in the Netherlands where we assume the cutters would be based, and one in South Africa—the source of the leaks.’

‘The South African Liaison officer,’ said Stephen, ‘is Captain Kurt Meisner, whom I’ve worked with twice before on previous cases, but that was about drugs and not diamonds. The Dutch have appointed Brigadier Helena Van Houten to the case as their liaison officer.’

‘Oh excellent,’ said Sam, ‘another woman. Although I must say a Brigadier sounds awfully high up for just a liaison officer?’

‘I thought much the same,’ interjected Paul, ‘but I understand from Interpol that Brigadier is apparently Dutch for Sergeant. In fact we have a three-way conference call booked with Captain Meisner and Brigadier Van Houten for roughly half an hour's time. It would make sense if you two sit in on the call as you will probably be able to answer some of their questions better than we can.'

'No problem,' I smiled. 'It's nice to be included.'

'By the way, Stephen,' asked Sam. 'Now that we're officially on the case, can we claim our travel expenses instead of Michael and I having to subsidise the Metropolitan Police?'

'Yes, you can,' Stephen responded. 'In fact, give me receipts for your total expenses to date, including the South Africa trip and I'll get Interpol to reimburse you Michael.'

'Fantastic, Stephen, thank you.'

'I think the first thing Sam and I need to urgently do is personally check out Thaxted Property Holdings headquarters,' I said. 'I estimate it will take us about two weeks.'

'Would that by any chance be the Thaxted Property Holdings headquarters that just happens to be located in the Bahamas?' enquired Stephen with a smile.

'Oh,' I laughed, 'is that where they are? Silly me, I'd forgotten.'

'Seriously though you two, are you up for some more travel if it comes to it. You're obviously convincing as a married couple and could prove very useful to the investigation?'

'As the Queen frequently says,' answered Sam in her best regal voice. 'My husband and I only wish to serve the nation and its people in whatever way we can.'

'I'll take that as a yes then,' smiled Stephen, and we all laughed.

Twenty minutes later, the first connection came through and Brigadier Helena Van Houten was now appearing on the large TV monitor on the wall in Stephen's office. I estimated she was in her late twenties or early thirties, and she was an attractive looking lady with shoulder length brunette hair. Her English was perfect.

'Good morning, Superintendent, and to you too, Inspector,' she said.

'Good morning, Helena. Can I please suggest,' said Stephen, 'that we do away with using everybody's ranks during these conference calls—it will be much less formal and I think we'll probably end up getting more work done with a friendly feel to everything. Can I introduce to you Dr Samantha Clark, who we've known for years as Sam and she used to be our best police surgeon before she moved to the Algarve? This gentlemen is the well-known author and novelist, and Sam's partner in crime—Mr Michael Turner.'

'I think it's now partner in every sense of the word isn't it?' asked Paul.

Sam ignored Paul's question, but smiled coyly at him, which in fact answered his question.

'Good morning, Helena,' Sam and I said in perfect unity.

'Good morning to you both from rainy Amsterdam. I gather from my conversation with Paul last night that discovering the potential size of this crime ring is principally down to you two. Well done.'

'Oh, for goodness sake,' interjected Paul, 'don't praise them too much, Helena, it will go to their heads. We do however feel their help in this will be invaluable over the coming weeks, and to that end we've appointed them official consultants to the Metropolitan Police on this case. So you can say anything in front of them.'

'Excellent,' responded Helena.

At that point the large TV monitor pinged again, and a second video link appeared, that of Captain Kurt Meisner, a big built man with a short, reddish coloured beard. The screen was now split in two with Helena on the left and Kurt on the right.

'Good morning, Kurt,' said Stephen, 'and welcome to the party. May I start by introducing Dr Samantha Clark and Mr Michael Turner? Sam and Michael will both be working with us on this as official police consultants, and it was Sam and Michael that discovered the De Beers courier link when they visited Johannesburg last week.'

'Good morning one and all in London,' responded Kurt Meisner, 'and also a very good morning to you too Helena. We have worked together on a couple of previous cases, also diamond involved. As you all know De Beers supply most of the raw materials to the world, and Helena's countrymen are without doubt the best in the world at cutting and polishing, so it's only natural that our paths have frequently crossed.'

'Do you think there is a Dutch involvement here, Helena?' I asked.

'We don't know for sure at this stage Michael, but we think it's most likely. As Kurt just said, we have the best cutters and polishers in the world here in Amsterdam, and it would be logical for what appears to be the world's best diamond thieves to use only the best to get their end product to market, i.e., Dutch cutters.'

'Is that what you are thinking about Derek Simpson and his gang,' asked Sam, 'they are now the world's best diamond thieves?'

'Based on what little information we have at this stage,' said Stephen, 'we think the scale of their operation far exceeds anything we, or Interpol have ever come across before. If they've followed the same pattern as they did with Malcolm Tisbury for example, and I'm basically following your scenario here Michael, and like you making this up as I go along, they could have for example been tipped off about a delivery of uncut stones to a client in Hong Kong—let's call him Mr Fu Man Chu.' We all laughed at the Fu Man Chu name, but Stephen was continuing.

'Derek Simpson and co. travelled to Hong Kong and waited until the stones were delivered and signed for as they did with Malcolm Tisbury, and then Freddie killed Mr Fu Man Chu—the one and only witness to the crime. As far as De Beers are concerned, the delivery had been made and signed for by Mr Fu Man Chu, and therefore their interest in the stones has ended. The only person outside of De Beers that knew the stones had even arrived in Hong Kong—Mr Fu Man Chu was now dead and one assumes dumped somewhere, and the thieves and murderers were on a plane back to where they came from and thousands of miles away. The Hong Kong police like the Portuguese police in Malcolm Tisbury's case would just assume Mr Fu Man Chu was just the victim of another senseless killing, without even realising a massive theft had even taken place.'

'For all we know,' said Paul, 'Derek Simpson and co. could have been doing this ever since they left the UK. We have no way of knowing.'

'That all makes a lot of sense,' said Kurt. 'The important thing now though is to get a lot of background investigation work done, and most importantly without tipping off De Beers or the criminals involved.'

'Why De Beers?' asked Sam. 'Surely they would want to know about any and all dodgy dealings as much as we do, and help however they could?'

'Firstly,' replied Kurt, 'we don't know at this stage where the leaks and tip offs are coming from, or for that matter how high up the source is. Secondly, reputation means absolutely everything to a company like De Beers. They would shut down external access to everything and insist on internal investigations only if they thought we were interested in them. I may be going out on a limb here, but if you don't mind me suggesting this Stephen, do you think that Michael and Sam could possibly head back to South Africa and do some more of their investigative work trying to source the leak? I can give them as much back up as they'd need behind the scenes, and they already have credibility with Marius Van der Byl at De Beers. I'm afraid all South African Interpol officers and local police are known to the security people at De Beers, and they'd know an investigation was under way immediately if any of us were out in the open.

'Personally, I have no problem with that, assuming Michael and Sam are happy to go along with it,' said Stephen.

'If Sam is happy, then I'm happy,' I responded.

'Ah, sweet,' mimicked Paul.

Sam hit him quite hard on the arm and everyone laughed.

'OK,' said Stephen. 'We'll organise two flights to Johannesburg from this end.'

'No, sorry to interrupt,' interjected Kurt, 'but it would much better if Michael and Sam flew to Pretoria where our Interpol offices are based first. I can then spend a couple of days with Michael and Sam and fully brief them before they move on to Johannesburg.

'If you don't mind me muscling in, Kurt,' said Helena, 'I'd quite like to join you both out there. Nobody knows me in South Africa, and as an Interpol officer I can be a great help to Michael and Sam if they find themselves in trouble, and also liaise with you Kurt in Pretoria. I could for example pretend to be Sam's sister Helena, who is also looking to invest some money left to her or something like that.'

'Sounds good to me,' said Kurt, 'and it would be very useful to have Interpol fully involved at all times. I can't do that as I'm too well known out here, but Helena could.'

'Excellent,' said Stephen. 'As my hero the great Hannibal Smith frequently said in the best ever TV show, "The A Team—I love it when a plan comes together".'

Chapter Fifteen

The following day, Helena, who had flown to London from Amsterdam's Schiphol airport late the previous evening, met Sam and I at London's Heathrow airport. The three of us then flew on a British Airways 747 to Cape Town where we boarded a short internal flight to Pretoria. As per our previous visit, we booked into the Sheraton, the only difference being this time Interpol were picking up the bill instead of me. Sam and I both liked Helena the minute we met her, and she and Sam got on so well that after half an hour in their company anyone would happily believe they were sisters.

The weather was excellent and we wanted to give the impression of simply being holiday makers, so we got changed into swimming clothes and the three of us sat on sun loungers around the pool. We chose a quiet spot in the corner where nobody else was sitting and could overhear our conversation, but we could see anyone approaching us. A waiter immediately came over and we ordered three cold beers and once he'd delivered them, we started to chat over our strategy.

Pretoria and its thousands of Jacaranda trees

The massive Voortrekker Monument, Pretoria

The Cullinan diamond mine near Pretoria, where the largest diamond ever was discovered

Entrance to Interpol's headquarters, Pretoria

'Two things come to mind,' Helena started. 'If there are frequent thefts, as we all suspect there have been, then the information has to be coming from someone reasonably high up who has access to all the upcoming delivery information, and that's not going to be someone as lowly as one of the couriers. Anyway, as far as I understand it, the couriers only ever know about each individual job they are given out.'

'Agreed,' I said, 'and knowing that to be the case our feeling was that the person that dishes out those jobs surely has to go to straight the top of the list of suspects.'

'Exactly,' replied Helena. 'Do you know who that is or what he's like?'

'We know nothing about him other than his name which is Francois Viljoen,' answered Sam, 'and his job title which is Courier Manager for De Beers. I'm afraid we never met him on our last trip.'

'I think he has to be our prime suspect,' mused Helena.

'OK,' said Sam, 'so assuming he's our prime suspect, how the hell do we find out if he is the source and how he gets the information out?'

'I've been thinking about that as well,' answered Helena. 'I needed something to do on the flight to Cape Town while you two were off in dreamland and merrily snoring away.'

'I do not snore,' I immediately protested.

'Sorry dear,' interrupted Sam, 'but yes you do. You sound like a constipated camel once you get going. I have to say—it's not your most attractive feature and it's definitely not why I fell in love with you.'

Helena laughed as I ignored Sam's cruel comments about my nocturnal sleeping habits, and I cleverly brought us back to the subject of Francois Viljoen.

'You were saying, Helena?' I asked.

The two women just laughed.

'I was about to say that I'd been thinking about how whoever it is gets the information to his contact at the other end, and I decided that if it was me I'd use burner phones.'

'Sorry to show my ignorance, but what on earth are burner phones?' asked Sam.

This was one I thought I could answer and jumped in before Helena could reply.

'Technically, a burner phone is just a prepaid mobile phone or cell phone as Americans call them. However, burners are different in that criminals use them specifically for just one job and then they are disposed of. Since prepaid phones can be bought with cash, and without a contract, they're virtually impossible to track. So it's easy for people to use them for certain illegal activities and then simply dump the phone. When a phone is considered "burned" or too risky to use, the criminals just dump them and simply buy another pay-as-you-go device.'

'Excellent description, Michael,' said Helena. 'That's what I'd do.'

'So,' said Sam, 'if Francois Viljoen is the one passing out the information for example, he simply telephones his contact and tells them the details.'

'No, not necessarily,' replied Helena. 'Again, if it was me I'd never speak on the phone. If the mobile that he'd used was ever found by the authorities, the tech boys could pull up old conversations through the service providers who record everything, and then they could use vocal recognition technology and software to identify whose voice was on the phone. I'd avoid that possibility and use coded text messages. You simply type in the client's name, date, time and place of delivery, probably using a simple book code, and then send the text, dump the phone and buy a new one ready for the next job. Let's face it, you can buy a new phone for twenty euros these days, and there's no way of knowing who sent the text even if you have the phone it was sent from. After that it would be up to the thieves.'

'Sorry,' asked Sam again. 'What's a book code?'

Helena looked at me and waited for me to explain.

'Come on then, Hercule,' she smiled, 'do your stuff.'

'A book code is virtually impossible to break,' I began. 'You simply agree before an operation starts on the book, it could be the Thirty Nine Steps, or a guide to the Lake District—literally any book. You buy two copies and have one each. Each text is simply a series of numbers such as for example one hundred and forty seven, ten, twelve, nine-eleven etc. You then type out your text according to the code in your copy of the book. So the person receiving the text knows that firstly they have to turn to page one hundred and forty seven in the book, go to line ten, and then the first letter in the message is whatever letter is the twelfth on that line, etc., etc. If you don't know which book is being used it's impossible to break the code.'

'Got it. OK, so how do we find out if it is Viljoen?' Sam asked.

'Easy,' said Helena. 'Sam and I will keep him busy while Michael nicks his phone and copies down the information on it.'

'Gee thanks,' I said. 'I see you two get the easy bit. But even if I was able to read his texts, there's probably nothing suspicious on it as he probably uses burner phones and then throws them away.'

'Don't worry about reading his text messages, he'll wipe anything incriminating as soon as he's sent them, and that's not what we want anyway. Go straight to his telephone contact list, that's what we need. Whoever he's sending the messages to will be on that list somewhere. It may be Dominic St Clair, or it could be Caroline Chambers, or it could be direct to Derek Simpson. He may, and I certainly would, use code names of some sort instead of real names, but just make a note of all Spanish or English phone numbers. If it is him then the contact number we want will be on the list somewhere.'

'OK, assuming I can do that, how are you two going to distract him for the ten minutes or so I'll need to go through his phone and copy stuff down.'

'Tell me, Michael,' began Helena, 'if two attractive ladies such as Sam and myself invited you to lunch at their hotel, plied you with wine and then asked you to join them for a swim after lunch, and you saw them both in tiny bikinis, would you be keeping an eye on your mobile phone, or might you be keeping an eye on us, and therefore be just a tad distracted?'

'I see your point,' I replied. 'So the idea then is for you two to go and see Viljoen and then invite him to lunch?'

'No, that's too obvious,' answered Helena. 'You and Sam make an appointment to go back and see Marius Van der Byl again, but I'll come along this time as Sam's sister and prospective partner in the new business. My only concern for the new business will be the possible theft of our stones, which I'm really worried about as I'm looking to put thirty million pounds of my own money into the business. We'll ask if we could be reassured by the man who organises the deliveries before we sign up. Van der Byl's not going to lose eighty million pounds worth of new business by saying we can't meet the head of the couriers. After all, we are just two ladies looking for a bit of simple reassurance over lunch. You

Michael, then tell Van der Byl that unfortunately you can't join us and Viljoen for lunch as you have to head off for another meeting, and that way we ensure Viljoen never meets you. You come back to the hotel and wait by the pool for us. You nick his phone at some point, go to your room and copy everything you need. Then hand his phone in to reception saying that you found it on the floor near the entrance to the pool and assume someone has dropped it. Just make sure his phone is put back to the same page as when you first open it.'

'Wow,' said Sam. 'You're really good at this, aren't you?'

'Well it's what I do for a living and I guess it becomes easy. I suppose it's the same with you and doctoring. I wouldn't have a clue and any patient seeing me would probably die within the hour. Likewise, I'm sure Michael finds it relatively simple writing his books, and unlike him I wouldn't know where to start. Each to their own as they say.'

'Would it help,' I asked Helena, 'if I kept Van der Byl occupied and stopped him joining you girls for lunch? I could tell him I want to go over various payment details, which bank accounts to use, international bank transfer security, can we avoid taxes if we open an offshore account etc., and I'll point out that you two won't really be involved in all that, so he and I should discuss all that while you're off meeting Francois Viljoen.'

'Excellent idea, Michael,' replied Helena, 'again, he's unlikely to refuse. So can you give Marius Van der Byl a call and set up a meeting for around eleven-thirty or midday tomorrow. That will give us a chance for a brief chat with him, and then Sam and I can go and meet Viljoen and then drag him off for lunch and the pool. If he can't do tomorrow, make it Wednesday, but it must be around lunch time.'

'What do we do if Viljoen leaves his phone in the changing room locker?' asked Sam.

'Oh that one's easy. I'll ask Kurt to be on hand at the hotel tomorrow to unlock it for Michael, hang around and then relock it when he's finished.'

'Well if Kurt's going to be there,' I asked, 'couldn't he copy the phone details?'

'In case you hadn't realised, what we're proposing to do in copying someone else's phone details is illegal, not serious, but never the less illegal. Both Kurt and I are Interpol officers and we're not allowed to do even the slightest thing illegal. However, what we can do is accidentally on purpose protect you from being seen you while you copy the details. If you were to get caught it will simply be a slap on the wrist, but if Kurt and I get caught we'll both get thrown out of Interpol and never be able to work with the police again.'

I telephoned De Beers in Cape Town from my mobile and after giving my name to the receptionist got straight through to Marius Van der Byl.

'Marius, good morning, it's Michael and Sam Peters.'

'Ah, Michael, good morning and how is London—having good weather I hope?'

'I've no idea to be honest Marius, we left London yesterday and Sam and I are back here in South Africa. When we got home we got talking to Sam's sister Helena about the proposed new business, and she got as excited about it as we are and asked if she could join us in the new company. She would like to invest an additional thirty million pounds of her own money, and we thought the only thing to do was pop over and chat it all through with you.'

'That's wonderful news, Michael. When did you wish to meet up?'

'Any chance the three of us could see you around midday tomorrow. We have a meeting with the bank early on, but we could be free any time after eleven thirty.'

'No problem, Michael. Midday it is. You remember where my office is alright?'

'Yes I do. One small thing, Marius, Helena is even more paranoid than Sam about courier security with such vast amounts of money involved. I told her all about the host of security systems De Beers have in place, but she still has some worries. Is there any chance both the girls could meet up with your Courier Manager?'

'Our Courier Manager? Yes of course the ladies can meet him, I see no reason why not.'

'You know what women are like Marius, but there's nothing like hearing reassurance from the horse's mouth so to speak, and I'm sure he will be able to answer any questions they may have, and totally calm their nerves. What's he like by the way, because I don't want to cause any problems if he's likely to be upset by the girl's silly paranoia?'

'Oh don't worry, there's no problem there Michael. Francois Viljoen is a very experienced man who has been with us many years. I'll let him know to join us.'

'Oh thank you, Marius. Look, I tell you what, why don't you and Mr Viljoen join the three of us for lunch tomorrow and let us return the favour. You paid the bill last time, now it's our turn to offer you some hospitality.

'Well thank you, Michael. Francois and I will look forward to seeing you tomorrow.'

I ended the call with Van der Byl, then booked three rooms at the Westcliff hotel where we had stayed on our previous visit. Helena had now telephoned Kurt and asked him to join us in Cape Town. We packed, left the Sheraton with Helena having paid the bill, and the three of us caught the next flight to Cape Town.

Chapter Sixteen

Kurt had checked straight into his room under the name of Jan Coetzer, and once the three of us had dumped our luggage, we joined him in his room. Helena explained the plan to Kurt who came up with a much simpler solution to the locker problem. He disappeared for about thirty minutes and then returned with a locker master key.

'How the hell did you get hold of that?' I asked.

'Simple. I went to the men's locker room, found the elderly cleaner and showed him my Interpol badge. I said we'd had a tip off that there were drugs in one of the lockers and I needed to borrow his master key in order to check the lockers. I swore him to total secrecy on pain of death, scaring the life out of him in the process, and told him to disappear for half an hour and then come back. As soon as he'd gone I nipped out to the hardware shop round the corner and got a copy cut. When I got back I went and found the cleaner and returned his key saying it had been a bad tip, but even so, he had to keep the search to himself. I gave him a hundred rand to keep quiet, which I will of course charge to expenses. We now have a key to every locker in the hotel, and they have no idea we have it.'

'Brilliant,' said Sam, 'thanks Kurt.'

'I think it's important,' said Kurt, 'that Helena maintains her disguise as Sam's sister, and that nobody discovers you are with Interpol, so even though I can't imagine you will need me, I will nevertheless hang around for another 24 hours until Michael has got the information. Can I suggest Michael that you bring Viljoen's mobile to my room, and I can then tell you what to do if you have any problems getting into it? He's probably got a password installed, or maybe even a fingerprint sensor, but I know how we can bypass that. I will happily oversee the copying, although I cannot actually touch the phone myself.'

'Thanks Kurt, that makes me feel much better.'

'I don't suppose we have any idea what make of mobile Viljoen has?' asked Kurt.

'No idea,' said Sam and Helena more or less in unison.

'You two are becoming freakily and scarily similar,' I said. 'Actually Kurt, thinking about it, Van der Byl was using an iPhone when we went to lunch with him last week. I noticed it because he left it laying on the table at the polo club during lunch, and I remember saying I'd got the same phone and how good it was. I'm pretty sure he said something about iPhones being standard issue from the company.'

'Well in that case once we've got our hands on it we can simply link Viljoen's phone to yours, and then copy his contact list straight into your phone. Apple will tell you it can't be done as it's part of their client information protection protocols etc., but in reality Interpol officers know all sorts of ways of doing things the big companies assure you can't be done.'

'Great,' said Sam. 'Well if it's going to be that simple and that quick, are sure you still need Helena and me parading our half-naked bodies in front of Viljoen?'

Kurt and I just looked at each other and then smiled.

'Oh, I think that's going to be absolutely essential,' laughed Kurt.

The three of us left Kurt in his hotel room and arrived at De Beers about five minutes before noon. It was a beautiful summer's day, and perfect weather for suggesting a cooling dip in the hotel swimming pool after lunch. Sam had booked a table for three in the hotel's dining room and I was primed with lots of banking questions having spent the previous hour with the manager of the largest Cape Town branch of Barclays Bank. Barclays used to be known as ABSA which stands for Amalgamated Banks of South Africa, but it is now a South African subsidiary of Barclays Bank PLC. We chose Barclay's not only because it is a financial services provider, offering both personal and business banking, credit cards etc., but it is a name British investors would feel familiar with and it was therefore the logical choice.

We went straight into Marius Van der Byl's office and after he had welcomed both Sam and myself back, we introduced him to Helena.

'Good afternoon Miss Peters,' he began, but Helena stopped him in his tracks.

'Oh please, I've just heard you call Michael and my sister by their first names, so please call me Helena, and if you have no objection I'll call you Marius?'

'I'd be delighted Helena, and welcome to De Beers. Can I get you all some coffee?'

'Do you have any tea?' asked Helena.

'Of course, I always forget about the British love of tea.'

Van der Byl picked up the phone from his desk and ordered a pot of tea for four.

‘Now ladies, I understand you still have some possible security concerns over how we transport our stones to the UK, and that you would like to meet with Francois Viljoen, our Courier Manager?’

‘I’m afraid that’s my fault,’ said Helena.

‘Both Michael and I have assured Helena that you have excellent security measures in place,’ said Sam, ‘but then Helena started asking all sorts of questions we couldn’t answer.’

‘I’m so sorry, Marius,’ began Helena, ‘but it all stems from my childhood. My parents gave me a beautiful necklace of emerald coloured stones and imitation diamonds for my eleventh birthday, and although in reality it wasn’t particularly valuable, it was to me because it was a gift from my parents. But it was stolen and I never saw it again. Ever since then I’ve had this paranoia as Sam calls it about security.’

‘Oh don’t worry, Helena. You’re not the first person to be worried about possible theft. I’ll give Francois a call and ask him to join us now before we all go to lunch.’

‘Ah, about lunch,’ I said. ‘Sorry to be a bit of a damp squib Marius, but we’ve just been at a very lengthy meeting with the manager of Barclays bank here in Cape Town, and I’ve got loads of paperwork to complete and account information I need to get from you prior to us transferring the deposit funds. I was hoping you and I could get all that done while the girls take Francois to lunch if you don’t mind. It’s the girls that have the questions which I’m sure Francois can easily answer, and if you don’t mind I’d like to get all the banking paperwork done prior to us flying back to the UK tomorrow.’

'Not at all, Michael. I've heard Francois talk about security so many times I could probably recite it all in my sleep.'

'Well if we can get through everything quickly enough, we can always join them for dessert and drinks.'

'Excellent,' exclaimed Van der Byl, who was I'm sure quite disappointed at not having lunch with two attractive ladies, but was instead going to be stuck with me and a host of very boring bank forms instead. To be honest I would rather have been with the girls, but needs must as they say.

'I'm afraid I've left some of the forms we'll need in the car, Marius,' I said.

'Give me ten minutes and I'll be right back.' I quickly made my exit and only just avoided a man approaching down the corridor. I shot into the open lift door and turned my back to the doors until he had passed. I peeped round the corner and saw him stop outside Van der Byl's office. I then headed for the ground floor and hid behind an open newspaper in reception. Back upstairs there was a knock on Van der Byl's door and Francois Viljoen entered. From what little I had seen of him he looked to be about forty-five'ish, had short hair, already going slightly grey, but he looked to be fit and healthy. As with everyone we had met at De Beers, he was wearing a very expensive tailored suit, white shirt and striped tie.

'Francois,' began Van der Byl, 'can I introduce you to Sam and Helena Peters who as I explained to you yesterday are over the coming years going to be doing a lot of business with us. I'm afraid Sam's husband Michael has had to go and collect some papers.'

Viljoen shook the two girl's hands and introduced himself. He was extremely polite.

'I hope you don't mind, Francois, but there is a slight change of plan,' said Van der Byl. Michael and I have a mountain of banking paperwork to complete, so if it's OK with you, it will be just yourself and the two ladies for lunch.'

'I hope you don't mind, Francois,' began Helena, 'but we've booked a table at our hotel for lunch—the food there is to die for. And then instead of sitting having coffee after lunch while we continue to harangue you with what you will I'm sure think are very silly questions, we thought it might be nicer to chat in the pool with cocktails instead. Will that be alright with you, Francois?'

'I have always been encouraged by De Beers to work on the principal that the customer is always right. If I have to I'm sure I can force myself to spend a little time drinking cocktails with two beautiful ladies in a swimming pool instead of sitting round a table in a suit and tie.'

'Super,' oozed Helena. 'Why don't you shoot off then and get your swimming things and we'll meet you outside the front of the building? We can leave the boring men to discuss their boring paperwork and their equally boring bank forms.'

I'd been sitting in reception for about five minutes when the lift bell sounded and Sam and Helena both emerged and headed out to our hire car. Sam had the keys in her handbag. Helena came straight back into the reception area a minute later, and totally ignoring me she then she stood and waited by the lift doors. Two minutes later the bell sounded again and Viljoen emerged. Helena went straight up to him and slipped her arm through his and as they left reception I heard her saying,

'Now tell me Francois, how on earth you will stop some group of nasty, horrible thieves stealing my extremely expensive diamonds?' I didn't catch his reply or anything else that was said as they went out through De Beers's revolving doors, and then Viljoen and Helena both climbed into the back of the car. Helena was obviously going to play the flattery card to the full and simply use Sam as her chauffer.

As soon as they'd driven off I shot back upstairs to Van der Byl's office and spent the next hour getting account numbers, setting up passwords, setting up on-line communications etc.

By five past one we had completed all the forms, but the last thing I wanted was Van der Byl coming with me, so I made my excuses about having to go back to the bank and suggested we met for a meal that same evening. Van der Byl jumped at that and I said I would phone him later with details. I left his office and got a taxi to our hotel. I changed into my swimming things and then found a sun lounger near the girls.

Sam wandered close by and said, 'His mobile must be in his locker- number 621 according to his wristband,' and she then went into the ladies changing room. Helena was still flirting like mad with Viljoen, although nothing had happened between them as far as I could see other than a lot of jovial banter. I left the poolside and went straight to the men's changing room, got my master key out and opened locker number 621. Sure enough sitting on the little shelf at the top was Viljoen's mobile. I noted how it was positioned, then pocketed the phone, relocked it and later shot up in the lift to Kurt's room. I knocked on the door and Kurt opened it immediately.

'Here you go,' I said as I showed him both my phone and Viljoen's. Kurt quickly gave me a white Apple cable and told me to connect the two mobiles together. Kurt then gave me a lot of detailed instructions that enabled us to bypass Viljoen's security code, and he then told me to press various combinations of buttons on both phones, and before I knew it, the entire contents of Viljoen's phone had suddenly been transferred to mine. Kurt then unplugged my phone and using the same cable, attached my phone to an Apple laptop he had brought with him, and everything he'd just copied onto my phone was now transferred onto his laptop.

'Couldn't you have just done that in the first place?' I asked.

'Yes I could, but if this case ever gets to court I can honestly stand up and testify that I've never touched Viljoen's mobile in my life. I know it sounds daft, but I have to protect both myself and the evidence.'

I put Viljoen's phone back to the page it was on when we opened it, and then I rushed back downstairs to the men's changing room, wiped the phone with a clean handkerchief and carefully put his mobile back exactly how I'd found it. I secured his locker with the master key and then walked back past the girls giving Sam a thumbs up that it was all done. I then headed to our room and got changed into a pair of light blue slacks and a white tee shirt.

Sam returned to our room five minutes later having left Helena with Viljoen, and she got changed whilst telling me what a slime ball Viljoen was. Helena and Kurt joined us in our room about fifteen minutes later with Helena now having got rid of Viljoen. Helena had told him she had obviously drunk too much wine, although most of it had ended up in a pot plant when he wasn't looking, and that as a result she now had a terrible head and was starting to feel dizzy. She begged him to forgive her, gave him a peck on the cheek and headed up to her own room where she had changed out of her bikini and into a bright yellow sun dress.

‘Well I’ve got all sorts of information from our friend Viljoen’s phone,’ announced Kurt. ‘I’ve got telephone numbers in Holland, the UK, Spain, Dubai, Venice and the Bahamas.’

‘Oh, I think Sam and I ought to go and check that last one out as soon as possible,’ I said and the other three laughed.

‘Seriously though,’ said Kurt, ‘this could be an absolute gold mine of information. If we are finished here in Cape Town for the time being, can I suggest we all go to my HQ in Pretoria where we can check out exactly who all these phone numbers belong to. My gut feeling is that Viljoen probably is the leak—it can’t just be a coincidence that he’s got phone numbers for most of the places where Thaxted have offices. He’s got to be the leak.’

‘You’re right, Kurt,’ said Sam. ‘It has to be him, and definitely if it turns out he’s got phone numbers for Derek Simpson or Dominic St Clair etc. in his phone.’

‘As well as his phone’s contact list,’ said Kurt, ‘I’ve also downloaded all his text messages, but I very much doubt if we’ll find anything there. I’m positive a guy as bright as Viljoen will have used burner phones.’

‘If he’s that bright how come we’ve managed to get all his contacts?’ I asked.

‘Well he has to keep them somewhere, and I don’t suppose it occurred to him for a minute that we’d suspect him and hack into his phone. If I say so myself what we’ve just done was pretty slick. Well done everyone.’

‘I think a special award should go to the lovely Helena who had to be all smarmy with that sleaze ball for most of the afternoon.’

‘As you British say: Shucks, it was nothing!’ exclaimed Helena.

'Er, sorry Helena, we don't actually say that,' I corrected her. 'That's the Americans.'

'Brits, Americans, it's all the same isn't it?' she asked with a smile.

'Wash your mouth out, young lady,' I retorted with a smile.

We separated, with Helena and Kurt going back to their rooms to pack, and forty-five minutes later the four of us were all checked out of the hotel, and waiting at the airport for the evening flight back to Pretoria.

Chapter Seventeen

We had agreed to meet up the following morning at Interpol's office in Pretoria, and at 10:00 am sharp Helena, Sam and myself were ushered into Kurt's office.

'Good morning my intrepid band of super sleuths,' said Kurt who was looking extremely pleased with himself.

'You're sounding very jovial,' said Sam. 'Good news on the mobile front I assume.'

'Yes, great actually. Please, sit yourselves down, I've ordered some tea and biscuits as soon as reception informed me you'd all arrived.'

Kurt had taken us into a private conference room with a large table in the centre, and ten comfortable leather chairs positioned around it. There were a couple of laptops and half a dozen telephones on the table, and a large TV screen on the wall at the end.

'OK,' began Kurt. 'Don't bother to write any of this down as I have it all summarised and printed up for you to take with you. Sam, you were spot on just now when you said good news on the mobile front. Viljoen's phone was an absolute treasure trove of information. I won't bother to go through the details of how we found out all of what I'm about to tell you, other than to say it involved a lot of phone calls and investigation through the night by a team of six officers.'

'Have you had any sleep at all, Kurt,' asked Helena, 'or have you been here all the time?'

'None, but I'm going to brief you all and then I'm heading home for a bit of shut eye. Right, firstly Viljoen is definitely the source of the leaks. In his phone we found contact numbers for Dominic St Clair, Derek Simpson, Caroline Chambers and Jeremy Green, all of whom we know, plus Hannes de Jaeger, a top diamond cutter based in Amsterdam who we suspect is the guy they use for creating new pieces out of the stolen stones. He used to work for one of the top companies in Amsterdam, but then he dropped out about ten years ago, and we think he's worked solely for Simpson ever since.'

'God, do you think it goes back that far,' I asked.

'Yes, I'm certain of it,' replied Kurt. 'De Jaeger's work always earned top dollar for his company, and he is just the sort of person Derek Simpson would need. Now as well as gaining a lot of telephone numbers, those numbers have led us to a lot of addresses and other information. Both Dominic St Clair and Derek Simpson live in the Spanish town of Mijas. We went onto Google Earth and zoomed in on Simpson's villa, and from what we can see, he has a large estate in the hills just outside Mijas, and the entire property is surrounded by a two metre high wall. There appear to be CCTV cameras everywhere and there are also a couple of goons wandering about. One is Jimmy Priestly, Simpson's chauffer, and the other is Alex Donovan, who is basically some muscle when needed. However, there was no sign of Freddie Drayton anywhere and we have no phone number or address for him. I'm afraid his location is still a total mystery.'

'Shit,' I said. 'Sorry girls, but that's the murdering bastard we want most.'

‘Oh don’t worry Michael, we’ll find him. Now, two interesting things about Jeremy Green and Caroline Chambers. As I said, I won’t bother to go into how we got all this information, but I promise you—this is all fact.’

‘You make it all sound incredibly intriguing,’ said Sam.

‘Well to be honest—it is. Fact number one for you. Jeremy Green and Caroline Chambers are brother and sister, well in fact, half brother and sister. They both have the same mother, a lady named Gwenda Greenberg, but she died from severe bronchitis about eight years ago. Jeremy’s father was Cyril Greenberg, who owned and ran a very successful printing business in Cambridge, England, but for some reason, and we don’t know why, when Jeremy grew up he changed his name by deed poll taking just the Green bit of his father’s name. All with me so far?’ asked Kurt, and after receiving a series of nods and yes’s from around the table he continued.

‘Fact number two. Gwenda Greenberg started life as Gwenda Chambers, but then she married Cyril and became Gwenda Greenberg. She’d had a few secretarial jobs after leaving school, but then things changed when she became Derek Simpson’s PA for his building business shortly after she’d married Cyril, and it was during this period that Caroline was born. We’re pretty certain that Gwenda was Derek’s mistress as well as his PA, and that Caroline Chambers is in fact Derek’s illegitimate daughter. Caroline was given her mother’s maiden name, and six months later Cyril and Gwenda were divorced.’

‘My God,’ said Sam. ‘What a tangled web some people live in. This is all amazing.’

‘Fact number three. Thaxted Property Holdings is as you know an offshore company based in the Bahamas. This has several advantages as the Bahamas derives its revenue from import tariffs, product sales taxes, licence fees, property and stamp taxes, but there is no income tax, no corporation tax, no capital gains tax, and no wealth tax. Again as you already know, Thaxted has just two shareholders and two directors in Jeremy Green and Caroline Chambers, but we have also discovered that Thaxted was originally based in Switzerland. This was long before the Swiss started opening their dealings to and started cooperating with the police, and in those early days the company was named Simpson Property Holdings, and it had just one owner and sole director—Derek Simpson. When the company moved to the Bahamas, Derek appointed Jeremy and Caroline as directors, and then after a few months he resigned as a director. Three months later he officially handed his shares on a fifty-fifty basis to Jeremy and Caroline. However, it is our firm belief that he is still very much the power behind the throne, and having checked out and valued all the property owned by Thaxted around the world, our conservative estimate is that over the last ten years he and the company have turned stolen diamonds into property worth over seven hundred million pounds.'

'Fact number four, and I have to say, this is the most worrying.'

'Grief,' I said. 'How much worse can it get?'

'I said this was fact number four, but in fact this is just a suspicion at this stage, although we're pretty sure our suspicions are correct. We now firmly believe that not all the income from stolen stones is being turned into property, but that Derek Simpson has now moved on to one of the most profitable commodities in the world—supplying arms to terror groups in the Middle East through Thaxted's office in Dubai. As I said, we can't prove it yet, but we are well on the way to doing so.'

‘This has become so much bigger than it started out, and I suspect our involvement is about to come to an end?’ I said.

‘Not at all,’ replied Kurt. ‘All the information we’ve shared with you this morning has naturally been fed upstairs, and because of my involvement from the beginning I’ve been appointed the senior case officer, and as such I can use whoever I want. There is still an awful lot of investigative work to be done behind the scenes that we can’t do ourselves. Interpol may be a worldwide organisation, but the force in each country is quite small and criminals worth their salt know who we all are and have our faces ingrained in their memories. If anyone gets wind that Interpol are involved, people like Simpson will just shut down his operations and we’ll get nowhere. So, if you are still happy to be involved, then you guys can still play tourists or business people and we can still use you to obtain information, although I should warn you, you may have to risk life and limb by pretending to be tourists in the Bahamas and checking out Thaxted Property Holdings. I hate asking you both, but someone has to do it.’

‘Oh no, really. Don’t you have something less horrible we could do,’ said Sam with a massive grin on her face.

‘I could still play Sam’s sister,’ said Helena, obviously keen to visit the Bahamas.

‘Sorry Helena, but we need you back in the Netherlands checking out what you can on Hannes de Jaeger and how he fits into the operation. Don’t forget, without him there are no finished products to sell and therefore no income. I’ll be working on the arms side of things from here, and all I ask is that everyone keeps in touch and let me know what is happening. Michael, all joking aside, can you and Sam head back to the Algarve, and then once I’ve set everything up I’ll give you a call and details of what we’ll need you to find out in the Bahamas. You'll have to fly to Miami first and then get a flight to the Bahamas from there, so can you please make sure you've both got an up to date ESTA.

'I've got one,' I replied, 'but I don't know about Sam.'

'I've never been to America,' said Sam. 'What on earth is an ESTA?'

'It's the application form for the USA Visa Waiver Program,' I said, 'and without it you won't get into the States. But don't worry, you can easily get one online.'

'Right,' said Kurt. 'I'm going to link us in to Superintendent Colshaw in London for a TV conference call and bring him up to date. If you can wait until that conference call has finished, then you guys can head back to your hotels, pack and return to Europe.'

Kurt and Stephen Colshaw spoke for about twenty minutes as Kurt brought the London end totally up to date. The three of us bid our farewells to Kurt and then Sam, Helena and I returned to our hotel and packed. We left our hire car at the airport and all caught the next flight to Cape Town, where we said our goodbyes to Helena who boarded the KLM flight to Schiphol. Sam and I got the BA flight to London Heathrow about an hour later, and then an Easy Jet flight to the Algarve. We were absolutely exhausted and virtually slept through the following day, before Sam checked in with Jan to ensure she hadn't lost all her patients.

Chapter Eighteen

Kurt didn't contact us for nearly a week, which was great because it gave us plenty of time to recover from what had been an exhausting trip to South Africa, and it also gave Sam time to see most of her patients. I spent a lot of my time swotting up on the Bahamas in preparation for our visit, and I was amazed at some of the things I discovered. For example, I thought the Bahamas was just two or three small to medium size islands. But no, I was totally wrong. The Bahamas is what's known as an "island country" consisting of over 700 islands, cays, and islets in the Atlantic Ocean, all southeast of the US state of Florida. Its capital is Nassau which is on the island of New Providence, but we would be heading for Grand Bahama which was where Thaxted Property Holdings had its headquarters.

According to my research, the Bahamas became a British crown colony in 1718, when the British clamped down on piracy, and then after the American War of Independence was over, Britain resettled thousands of Americans that had been loyal to Britain in the Bahamas. Over the following years the Bahamas became a haven for freed African slaves, until slavery itself was abolished in the Bahamas in 1834. Today the descendants of slaves and freed Africans make up nearly ninety percent of the population. The Bahamas eventually became an independent realm, although still part of the commonwealth in 1973, retaining Queen Elizabeth II as its monarch. In terms of GDP, or Gross Domestic Product for the less politically or financially minded, the Bahamas is now one of the richest countries in the Americas, second only to the United States and Canada, with its economy based on just two industries: tourism and offshore finance. As much as I respect Great Britain, I have to say the Bahamian economy has prospered amazingly since gaining its independence from Britain. Tourism as an industry not only accounts for over 60% of the Bahamas income, but it also provides jobs for more than half the country's workforce. After tourism, the next most important economic sector is banking and offshore international financial services, and this was where Thaxted Property Holdings came into the picture.

Kurt eventually called eight days after we had left South Africa. Sam was with me at the time, and I put my mobile on speaker so I didn't have to repeat anything to her.

'Hi you two,' he began. 'I'm really sorry for the delay in getting back to you, but we needed to put together a complete wish list of what we would like you to find out for us if possible. We've now done that and I'm emailing the list over to you now. Tell me, how soon could you get away and start nosing around?'

'I guess we could set off tomorrow if it's urgent,' Sam replied on our behalf.

'But ideally we'd prefer another twenty-four hours to get packed and sort ourselves out.'

'Twenty four hours is fine,' responded Kurt. 'I'll leave you both in peace for now. Go through the wish list from the email and I'll call you back first thing tomorrow morning.'

'Thanks Kurt—talk soon,' I said and the line went dead.

Kurt's "wish list" was going to give us plenty to do. He wanted to know who else worked for Thaxted and if possible for us to get a complete list of employees and their phone numbers. He also wanted a complete list of all the properties they owned round the world, who they banked with, if there was more than one bank, which branches, contact names, account numbers and a complete list of where all the income had come from over the last ten years.

'Well that lot will help pass the time away,' said Sam in a very sarcastic voice. 'How the hell are we supposed to get all this sort of information?'

'The same way you approach any list I guess,' I replied, 'you do it one thing at a time. I guess the first thing we need to do is to book our flights and find ourselves a hotel on Grand Bahama, but it'll have to be the best hotel on the island in order to keep up the cover of our being filthy rich, and with nothing to do except travel the world spending money.'

'If only,' sighed Sam.

I did quite a bit of research on the internet and eventually booked us into the Grand Lucayan Resort Bahamas. It was quite a large hotel, but I worked on the principle of wanting lots of people around if anything got nasty, not that I was expecting any trouble, but we were going up against people who didn't think twice about murder. I then booked our flights. Easy Jet to London, British Airways to Miami and then a short island hopper plane run by American Airlines from Miami to Freeport. Two days later Sam and I checked into the Grand Lucayan.

Opposite the hotel was Port Lucaya market, which has over a hundred little shops selling everything a tourist could think of, from cheap tee shirts to forty thousand pound designer watches. As well as the shops, there was a host of restaurants and bars, and after we'd had a good lunch we headed off to take a look at Thaxted Property Holdings headquarters. It was certainly an impressive building. It was a three storey rectangular building, with a three storey foyer sticking out of the front centre of the building. The foyer had four fluted columns going from the ground to the triangulated foyer roof. All the walls were painted sky blue, meanwhile the roof, all the building trim, and all the columns and shutters either side of every window were painted white. The building sat back from the road in about an acre of beautifully manicured, lush lawn, all edged with flower beds full of bright red, yellow and purple flowers. Thaxted Property Holdings headquarters building was without doubt one of the most wonderfully proportioned and well balanced colonial style properties we had so far seen on the island, and it certainly looked to be worth millions.

We had no intention of going inside the building on the first day, but we parked our hire car a couple of streets away, and went for a walk. We walked round the building holding hands and I took several photographs of Sam posing in front of the building, mainly in order to have a good photographic record of all four sides of the building. In addition, we also ensured that we took plenty of photographs of Sam standing with several other buildings in the background, just to alleviate any suspicion in case anyone happened to be watching us.

After our evening meal which we ate in one of the hotel's four restaurants, we walked back to Thaxted's to see if there was anyone on the premises overnight, and to see if there was any obvious security in place. The building was in total darkness with no sign of security either.

‘I have no idea what’s inside the building,’ said Sam, ‘but I would imagine it’s just lots of property details and photographs, plus your usual office paperwork.’

‘Well they sure aren’t going to keep large amounts of cash on the premises when the island has so many banks, including one next door,’ I replied.

Fidelity Bank (Bahamas) Ltd had an equally large and impressive building located next door to Thaxted’s, except their building was cream and white.

‘Let’s wander round the back,’ I suggested. ‘Just to see if there are any obvious alarms.’

‘Why the hell would we need to know that?’ asked Sam. ‘You’re not thinking of breaking in are you?’

‘Well we can hardly go in and ask them for all the information we need. To be honest I don’t think we have an alternative, and if we aren’t prepared to give it a go, what the hell are we doing here. I am of course open to alternative suggestions if you have any?’

‘Sorry Michael, it’s just my natural instinct for self-preservation kicking in. It just never occurred to me until you just said it that we’d need to burgle the place, and having a criminal record is not something I’m looking to achieve in life.’

‘I’m not suggesting we do anything now, but I suggest we come back in the morning, chat to someone about acquiring a fantastic property somewhere in the world, and try and gather as much info as we can about the company and the building without making them suspicious. If we’re going to need the help of a professional to get in, then I’ll telephone Kurt and ask him to put his best burglar on the next flight out.’

We had a brief wander round the building, could see no movement and no alarms, and then we returned to the hotel where we sat in the bar and chatted to a lovely couple from Kent who were simply on a pleasant relaxing holiday. If only our life was that simple at the moment!

The some of the small shops in Port Lucaya Market, Bahamas

The Grand Lucayan Resort, Bahamas

One of the many buildings in Freeport, the same design as Thaxted's HQ.

The beach as Port Lucaya, Bahamas

Chapter Nineteen

We ate a really good cooked breakfast around 9:30 and at 11:15 am, we set off and drove over to the Thaxted building, having talked through the plan we'd made the night before. Our hire car was a rather swish dark blue BMW seven series with a cream leather interior, but we had to create the right impression when we drove up to Thaxted's front door. We'd decided to dress in an expensive, though casual looking manner, and Sam was wearing a very expensive Stella McCartney white dress and matching jacket which she'd bought last year and it really showed off her blonde hair and Algarve tan. The ensemble was finished off with a pair of smart gold coloured Jimmy Choo shoes. I'd gone down the nautical theme with white slacks and white slip on shoes, a pale blue tee shirt and a navy blazer to finish the ensemble. We both wore expensive looking sun glasses that we'd purchased at Lucaya market the previous day.

We drove right up to reception, left the car outside their front door, and we were greeted by a well-dressed young lady as we entered the building.

'Good morning sir, good morning madam, and welcome to Thaxted Property Holdings. My name is Casandra and how can we help you?'

'Well good morning to you too, Casandra,' I replied. 'We're looking for another property, and we were both very impressed and very intrigued by your website. Lots of nice words and promises accompanied by lots of photographs of amazing properties, but no details on anything.'

'Well if we put everything on the website, sir,' she smiled, 'you wouldn't need to come and see us would you? Please take a seat and I'll get our property manager to come and speak with you.'

She pointed at a group of very comfortable looking armchairs and we collapsed into two of them. A gorgeous brunette in I estimated her mid-thirties descended the central half-moon shaped staircase and came over and introduced herself.

'Good morning to you both. My name is Naomi Gardiner, and I am Thaxted's Property Manager. Casandra tells me you're looking to purchase a property and are interested in what we have to offer. But before we get started, can I offer you a drink—champagne, wine or perhaps you would prefer tea or coffee?'

'I would love a glass of red wine if that's possible,' and I looked at Sam who nodded, and then I said, 'the same for my wife please. By the way, my name is Michael Philips and this is my wife Samantha, although everyone calls her Sam.'

'Please, let's go to my office where we can chat in private,' said Naomi. Are you both OK with the stairs or would you prefer the lift?'

'No, we're fine with a bit of exercise,' Sam responded.

We walked up the stairs chatting fairly mindlessly about life in England, and how we'd got totally fed up with the weather and decided to travel around until we'd found somewhere to settle and call home. We'd set up two fairly detailed personas with Kurt's help, and he'd put loads of information about Michael and Sam Philips on the internet, all of which backed up the tale we were telling. We got to Naomi's office and the three of us sat down in easy chairs surrounding a coffee table. Casandra brought in three large glasses of red wine and then we started chatting in earnest.

'Can you tell me a little bit about yourselves, Michael, and what sort of property you're after, and if you don't mind—your budget, and most importantly, where do you want to live?'

'Well to be perfectly honest Naomi, it's all inherited wealth. My father was the late Sir Colin Philips and he owned one of the largest and most productive oil fields in western Russia. When he decided to retire he sold out to a Russian Oligarch for an absolute fortune, and being his only child everything came to me and my wife when he sadly died last year.'

'Oh, I'm so sorry to hear that,' said Naomi, but you could almost see the pound signs ticking over behind her eyes. 'So how can I help—what sort of property are you looking for and what is your budget?'

'There isn't a budget figure as such,' said Sam, 'if the property is right well then it costs whatever it costs. The real problem is we don't really know what we want, or where we want it, and we won't do until we see it.'

'Do you have leaflets on your properties we could look through?' I asked.

'Oh, Thaxted Property Holdings can do much better than that,' said Naomi.

'Can I suggest we look through a few DVD presentations from our property portfolio, and if we do it country by country we can hopefully narrow the choice down? Can I ask where you live at the moment, and are you wanting the sun, mountains, scenery, history etc.'

'OK,' I began and then went through the story Kurt had put together for us.

'Well we have several properties at the moment. We have a very pleasant seven bedroom house in Berkshire in England that was my father's, but as I said, due to the terrible weather in England we hardly ever use it?' We also have an excellent large apartment overlooking the sea in Monaco and we love it there. I suppose you could say that's our main base at the moment. We do of course have a house in the States, just outside San Diego in a little town called La Jolla, I don't know if you've heard of it?'

'Oh yes, I've heard of La Jolla,' smiled Naomi.

La Jolla (pronounced Ler Hoyer) is one of the wealthiest areas of southern California, and your ordinary everyday millionaire simply couldn't afford to live there. Kurt had suggested we use it as a "throwaway line" to help create the right impression. There was no doubt—we were creating the right impression on Naomi.

'Last year we bought a ski lodge in Klosters, that's in Switzerland,' said Sam, 'but I suppose you knew that?'

Naomi just smiled as she nodded.

'We just love skiing,' continued Sam, 'and you meet such nice people at Klosters. Anyway, we'd always stayed at this nice hotel there previously, it's called the Waldorf, no that's not right, well it's something like that.

'Do you mean the Walserhof Hotel?' asked Naomi.

'Yes that's it,' enthused Sam. 'Aren't you clever knowing all these places,' said Sam.

'Well it's all part of my job,' said Naomi. 'As well as being able to offer clients exclusive properties, they have to be located in the right areas as well, so it's very important to have a good grasp of the world's best places to live.'

'Anyway, as I was saying, we couldn't get into the hotel last time we wanted to, I think some prince or other had moved in, and we didn't want to risk that again, so when we saw this really nice ski lodge for sale we bought it.'

'So,' said Naomi. 'You have your home in England, two places in the sun, with one in Monaco and one in La Jolla, and you have a mountain retreat in Klosters. Anything else?'

'Yes,' I said, 'we also have a nice beach front property in Cape Town which again we inherited from my father, but we've only been there once.'

'Ooh,' exclaimed Sam, 'don't forget the new villa on the coast in Dubai. We just love Dubai. We bought a gorgeous villa there—well at least it looked gorgeous in the brochure, but we don't know for sure as they haven't actually finished building it yet. We didn't get time to visit it on our last trip as it was all a bit of a rush and we had to get back to England as my elderly aunt was dying. It would have been a lot easier if we were staying in Dubai itself, but we were a bit further up the coast at the Hilton hotel in Raz something or other.'

'I think the hotel you meant was the Hilton at Ras Al Khaimah,' offered Naomi.

'Is there anywhere in the world you're not familiar with Naomi,' I asked in my most friendly and flattering voice.

'As my boss always says, if we don't know it, it's not worth knowing,' said Naomi.

'Now he sounds like someone I'd like to chat to,' said Sam, 'is he available to join us?'

'No, I'm afraid Mr Green is out of the country on business for a few days,' she replied, 'but I'm sure I can help you with whatever you need regarding a potential new property.'

So I thought, they're not trying to keep Jeremy Green's name a secret, which confirmed Kurt's assumption that

Jeremy Green was just a front for the real owner—Derek Simpson.

'I know this is asking a lot,' said Sam, 'but I don't suppose you've got one of those gorgeous old palaces located on the Grand Canal in Venice on your books?'

'Aah Venice,' cooed Naomi, 'my favourite city in the world. Do you know it well?'

'No, not at all to be honest,' said Sam, 'but it always looks so great on the television.'

'Well as it happens we do have a property in Venice. It's not a palace as such, but we do have a very large three story seventeenth century house located on a different large canal in Venice. If anything, I would say it is much better because you don't get millions of tourists outside your front door all through the summer, and this particular property also has its own private boat dock.'

'Ooh, that sounds wonderful,' squealed Sam. 'Do you have any pictures?'

'I can do much better than that,' said Naomi. 'I have an HD quality DVD of the property showing both the external facilities and all the glorious interiors.'

'If we are interested in the property,' I asked, 'do we then contact the owner to arrange a viewing, or do we arrange it through you.'

'That's the easiest question of all to answer,' replied Naomi. 'We don't represent any other owners—we own every property on our books ourselves, and everything is arranged through myself and our legal team. If after you've viewed the DVD you'd like to view the property, I will quite happily fly you both to Venice on our own private jet so that you can view the real thing. I promise you, you won't be disappointed. Come into the viewing room, which is a bit like a home cinema, and we'll view the property while Casandra opens another bottle of this excellent Cabernet Sauvignon.'

'Please forgive me for being really nosey, Naomi, but you must own a lot of properties around the world and I'm sure none of them are at the bottom end of the market. Until I saw your website I have to admit I'd never even heard of Thaxted. No TV ads, and you don't seem to advertise the company anywhere?'

'To be frank with you, Michael,' responded Naomi, 'with the average price of our properties being well in excess of ten million pounds sterling, there is no point whatsoever in TV or any other form of mass marketing. We try to source wealthy clients from around the world and we then offer them various incentives to purchase, or at least view potential properties for them.'

'If you don't mind us asking you, and I apologise if it seems rude, but just how many properties do you have on your books?' asked Sam.

'Not at all—we have no secrets.'

I didn't believe that for a minute, but I kept my mouth shut.

'At this moment in time,' she continued, 'we have one hundred and sixty three different properties in the portfolio. To save you doing the math, at an average value of eleven million pounds sterling, our current portfolio of property assets is worth approximately one point eight billion pounds.'

'Wow, it sounds like your Mr Green is an extremely wealthy man,' said Sam.

'Oh no,' exclaimed Naomi. 'Mr Green is my boss and he is far from poor, and I know he and his sister are the two shareholders of the company, but I'm pretty sure the real owner is someone else. I know this may sound crazy, but I really have no idea who that is as I've never managed to find out. For all I know I could be working for an American billionaire, an Indian maharajah or an Arab sheik, but as long as they continue to employ me and pay me I don't really care. I'm very happy not knowing. Now, let's have a look at this wonderful property in Venice.'

We spent the next hour and a half with Naomi viewing the DVD, and I have to admit, if I had a spare eighteen million pounds, which was the cost of this particular property in Venice, I would be sorely tempted to spend it. We learnt a lot from Naomi who freely admitted that while we were checking out Thaxted's various properties, Thaxted was checking out Sam and myself. Kurt had set us up on the internet so that any search for Michael and Samantha Philips went straight to our own website controlled by Kurt and his technical team in Pretoria. Kurt knew the moment anyone logged on and where they were from. He could also see what pages they were looking at, and any searches they were doing. We weren't concerned as we knew any search would show that Sam and I had inherited Sir Colin Philips entire estate worth in excess of eight billion pounds. According to all the various links Kurt had installed, Sir Colin had been quite a recluse and he'd shunned publicity all his life. Sam and I were being portrayed on the site as a couple of wealthy spendthrifts who were speedily working our way through our inheritance. Kurt had also put up a Wikipedia entry about our supposed family and one or two smaller entries about Sir Colin. All in all, there was plenty to satisfy Thaxted that we had plenty of money in the bank. We'd also casually dropped into the conversation that Sam was thinking of getting involved somehow with her favourite hobby—really expensive jewellery. She wasn't sure how yet, but she wanted to do something.

'Well what do you think?' asked Naomi after we'd finished the screening. 'Do you want to go and view the real thing? If so we can fly you both to Venice tomorrow and then view the property the following day. Casandra has rung through to say that you both passed all the financial checks with flying colours, and I'm sure you understand why we have to do so. If we didn't check out the wealth and status of all potential clients we could end up spending a fortune on complete time wasters.'

'We understand completely, Naomi,' I replied. 'I would be doing exactly the same thing in your position. Well speaking for myself, I loved the interiors of the Venice property, even if the outside is in need of a bit of TLC, and I'd would be quite happy to see the real thing. What about you Sam?'

'Can't you tell by the big grin on my face? Of course we should go and see it.'

'Fine,' exclaimed Naomi, 'well in that case I'll make all the arrangements and I'll pick you up from reception at the Lucaya at 9:30 in the morning. I should pack clothes for a couple of days. I'll also book us into a nice hotel in Venice.'

Naomi stood up indicating our meeting had come to a close.

'Is there anything else I can help you with at this stage?' she asked.

'I don't think so,' I replied, 'but just in case we do have any questions, will either you or someone be here this evening if we called in again. Sorry to ask, but you know what it's like, you always think of questions after you've left.'

'No, I'm sorry, Michael, we shut shop promptly at 6:00 pm every day, lock up and all go home. But here is my business card which has my cell phone number on it, and please feel free to call me anytime. If I don't hear from you I'll see you at your hotel in the morning.'

Around 4 pm, we drove back to the hotel, made lots of notes and listed what we still needed to find out. There was only one way to do that, and that was to break in overnight. We felt that was going to be the case yesterday, and I'd already spoken to Kurt about it. He said he was going to send Martin Smith—not being his real name of course—over to join us at our hotel in Freeport sometime in the late afternoon. I asked Kurt who Martin was, and he simply said Martin would assist us in solving our access to private information problems and we should rest assured as he was the best in the business.

To me that sounded like Martin Smith was a top class burglar.

Chapter Twenty

Martin duly arrived at our room around 4:30 pm, and I have to say he didn't look anything like a burglar, although to be honest I have no idea what a burglar should look like!

'Hi,' I began and introduced both Sam and myself.

'Hello,' said Martin as he entered our room. 'I assume Kurt has filled you in about me, and I'm happy to help, but it would be useful if you could tell me exactly what is needed?'

'Quite frankly, Martin,' I said. 'Kurt has told us absolutely nothing about you other than your name, which I gather isn't your name—if you see what I mean?'

'Typical Kurt,' laughed Martin. 'In that case let me fill you in. Kurt's always anxious about saying too much in case it puts people off. I hope that because Kurt's recommended me and paid for me to get here that you will trust his judgement?'

'No problem,' smiled Sam.

'Well my Christian name is Martin, that is genuine, but my surname certainly isn't Smith, and nobody other than Kurt and his immediate boss know what my real surname is. I'm thirty eight years old and if I say so myself, I'm without doubt the best burglar in South Africa, probably in all of Africa, and I'd certainly rate myself in the world's top ten.

Kurt and I met when I was on a bank job in Johannesburg, and an idiot I was working with tripped a silent alarm because he ignored my instructions. Both the local police and Interpol arrived, and to cut a long story short, Kurt took me aside and gave me a choice—fifteen years in prison or work for him. As you are obviously aware I chose the latter and I have now been working for Interpol for over six years. Kurt sends me out on jobs where they need access to a building that can't be done openly by simply walking through the front door. Interpol also pay all my expenses, plus a very good monthly retainer so that I'm not tempted back into my "evil ways" as Kurt calls it, during my spare time. Now, Kurt said he needs you two to get into a building and get out again with lots of information, but the building's owners must be totally unaware of our visit. Does that more or less sum it up?'

'I'd say that sums it up beautifully, Martin,' said Sam. 'However, neither Michael nor I have ever broken into a building in our lives. At least I haven't, and I don't think Michael has, and we certainly don't want to drop ourselves or you in it by making mistakes.'

'No Sam,' I jumped in. 'I've never broken into anywhere.'

'OK,' said Martin. 'Fill me in. Where are we breaking into and what are we after?'

We decided to chat over a pot of tea as Martin insisted no alcohol should pass any of our lips until the job was completed. We'd already agreed that whatever Martin said—we would obey. We then outlined the situation at Thaxted in detail, and told Martin about Kurt's information wish list.

One—obtain a complete list of all Thaxted's employees, their home and mobile phone numbers and all their email details.

Two—obtain a complete list of all the properties Thaxted owned around the world. Three—with whom do Thaxted bank, at which branches do they have accounts, what are the various contact's names, what are their various account numbers etc. and Four—obtain a complete list of where all the income had come from over the last ten years.

Some of the information we already had, for example we knew Naomi Gardiner was the Manager and that Casandra Dufreine, a local girl, was both the receptionist and Naomi's PA. We had seen a few other people in the building, but I had also seen a list next to the phone in reception of all the staff and their extension numbers. We also now knew where to get the complete list of all the properties they owned. Naomi had such a list, including the asking price for each property on the desk in her office. As for the rest of the info Kurt wanted? We had no idea.

'You said earlier,' began Martin, 'that you were flying to Venice tomorrow with Naomi on her private jet. Is that essential, or can you get out of it?'

'Well I guess we could say we'd changed our minds, but why?'

'Look, the more time you spend with these people the more likely you are to drop yourselves in it by saying something that makes them suspicious. Plus, from what you tell me, it's basically a jolly that will give you no more information about the company that I can't get for you from their computers. Why risk it?'

'Well I guess I could telephone Naomi, I've got her mobile number, and say we've changed our minds and want more time to think about it.'

'No, don't do that,' insisted Martin who then paused for thought. 'Instead of eating in one of the restaurants in the hotel tonight, let's grab something to eat from one of the fast food stalls across the road in Port Lucaya Market. Then Sam can get food poisoning and not be fit to fly tomorrow. You're obviously still very interested in the Venice property, but sadly will have to wait to visit it until Sam has fully recovered. Much less suspicious and it gives you time to leave the island and get back to Europe. I assume Naomi doesn't know your real names or where you live etc.?'

'No,' I replied. 'Kurt even insisted that we left our own mobiles behind in case anyone from Thaxted managed to sneak a look at them when we weren't aware. Instead he gave us new mobiles that only contained what he called "approved numbers", i.e., loads of different names and numbers so that the phones seem perfectly normal, but every call made to any of the contact numbers will apparently get routed to an Interpol desk who always answer in the appropriate person's name, and they each have a persona for that person ready at hand to chat if necessary.'

'That man never takes any chances,' said Martin. 'I have to say, he's the most thorough and impressive police officer I've ever come across. So, Sam, going back to eating—are you prepared to get violently ill with chronic food poisoning and possibly die for the cause?'

'Gee thanks, Martin! Look, I don't really have to get sick, do I? I mean, in real life I'm a bloody good doctor and I know what the effects of food poisoning looks like, so I could easily fake it if necessary.'

'No, of course you don't have to get sick in reality,' laughed Martin, 'but just to be on the safe side we have to assume you could be being watched, and therefore you can't say you have food poisoning if you've eaten in a top class restaurant as nobody else that ate there has become unwell.

You need to have eaten at one of the fast food places where it might be possible you've had a bad burger or something.'

'That's fine then,' said Sam breathing a sigh of relief.

'I suggest we head over to the market,' said Martin, 'grab a burger and chips or a hot dog and a lemonade or coke etc., and then head back here to the hotel and grab some shuteye. It doesn't matter if I'm seen with you by the way. They won't know me from Adam, and I'm booked in here under a cover name with an excellent Interpol legend, and a great backup story which I've used now for the last five years without a problem. We'll all meet up again at 1:00 am in your room, and then head off to Thaxted's headquarters in my beaten up old hire car.'

'Will we have to black up our faces?' asked Sam.

'No,' laughed Martin. 'I think you've seen too many heist movies Sam. No, just wear dark clothes, no bright yellow jumpers or white jeans.'

Chapter Twenty-One

Having dutifully eaten our burgers complete with greasy chips and grabbed a few hours shuteye, we headed off on the dot of 1:00 am with Martin at the wheel of an old dark green Renault he'd picked up from "Bob's Autos", a cheap and cheerful car hire company at the airport. It was very cheap, totally forgettable and just what was needed. Martin parked a couple of streets away and we walked to Thaxted's, approaching the building from the rear.

'OK you two,' said Martin, 'just wait here. Have a kiss and cuddle as cover in case anyone sees you, and I'll come back and pick you up when it's all clear.'

As previously agreed, we obeyed Martin to the letter, quite enthusiastically to be honest, until about twenty minutes later we heard a little cough and looked up to find Martin staring down at us lying on the grass behind a hedge. Sam and I both adjusted our clothing and stood up.

'Just obeying your instructions boss,' smiled Sam to Martin.

'Mmm,' he smiled back. 'Right, I'm in and I've dealt with the alarms. I can reset everything when we leave. There were basic contact alarms on all the windows, but I bypassed those easily enough and then got into the main alarm control box, which is now turned off, but I've attached a little box I brought with me that makes it think it's still working even though it isn't. Now when we get in, take me straight to Naomi's office, and we'll get what we can off of her computer. I've got a powerful little laptop in my bag of tricks and we'll just copy her entire files. While I'm doing that, you two can try and find the accounts department, but please don't touch anything until I join you.'

We quickly ran across the grass, and stood with our backs close to the wall. Martin put his bag of tricks as he called it on the grass and then slid up the small sash window. He asked me to enter first, followed by Sam and then Martin brought up the rear bringing his bag with him, and then he closed and locked the window behind him. I looked at him puzzled.

'Just in case a security patrol goes past and tries the window,' he said.

Now I freely admit, I wouldn't have thought of that, but then thank God, I'm not a full time professional burglar. It was pitch black inside the building and I couldn't see a thing, but again, it hadn't been much better outside. Every night in the Caribbean is pitch black once you are away from the street lights.

'Now just stand perfectly still and close your eyes. Count slowly to thirty and then open them again. You should find your night vision will have improved. We can't use torches in case they're seen by anyone from outside.' We did as Martin had told us, and when we opened our eyes again, we could initially see just rough shapes, but then as our vision improved we could see where desks and chairs were located etc.

'OK,' said Martin. 'Please take me to Naomi's office.'

I led the way up the stairs and turned right. Naomi's office was the first door. I was about to open her office door when Martin grabbed my wrist and stopped me. Martin walked past me and held some little box of electronics he'd taken from his bag against the door. He pushed a few buttons on the box, and the door to her office clicked.

'I could see from the main alarm box downstairs earlier that some of the offices had silent alarms fitted on the doors. That click you heard has just turned off the alarm and unlocked the door.'

'Thank God you're with us,' said Sam.

'I nearly dropped us all in it, didn't I?' I asked.

'Nearly, but fortunately not quite,' replied Martin. 'Don't worry about it. This isn't a job for amateurs. Just remember to do no more and no less than I tell you and we'll all be fine.'

'I'm glad you're so confident,' said Sam. 'Excuse my language but I'm shitting myself.'

'Well the ladies loo is just down the corridor,' I said.

'I'm speaking metaphorically, not literally, you prize moron,' laughed Sam, which helped break the tension. Martin opened the door and entered Naomi's office. We followed behind and Sam closed the door on Martin's instructions. Martin again run his little box of electronics all over Naomi's computer, clicking and pushing buttons as he went, and he then declared it was clean and pushed the power button to turn the PC on. Next, he walked over to another door in her office and after he'd checked it he opened it and went inside. He emerged a few seconds later.

'I assume you've both got your mobiles with you?' Martin asked.

'Yes,' I replied on behalf of both of us.

'You said there was a book with all the properties on Naomi's desk. Can you see it here?' Martin asked. I saw it and was about to pick it up. Again, Martin grabbed my wrist, and then spun me round so that my back was to her desk.

'Tell me Michael, is the book front cover up or down, is it touching any pens or pencils, is it covering any other books?'

'OK, I get it. I have no idea and I've nearly done it again. Sorry Martin.'

'Don't worry, this is my area of expertise and not yours, but please, both of you, as I said before—don't touch or do anything unless I ask you to.' Martin picked up the book and handed it to me. He then picked a fairly thin book of A4 paper sheets held together in a plastic binder from Naomi's desk and handed it to Sam.

'Right, while I'm sorting the computer you two can make yourselves useful. Through that door is a private shower and toilet, and fortunately for us it has no windows. Go in there taking the book and the phone list with you, shut the door tight and then turn the light on. Photograph every page on your mobiles, and when you've finished, turn the light off and then come back out here. Remember, only turn the light on once the door is shut tight, and turn the light off before you open the door to come out. Also, your night vision will be completely crap again, so do the same routine again before you come back into the office, you may even have to do it twice as you'll be coming from a bright light. Go.'

Sam and I went into the shower room and once the door was shut tight I turned the light on. At first I had to squint as the light seemed incredibly bright, but after ten seconds or so our eyes acclimatised and we started photographing. Sam's book was a telephone and contact list which had names, job titles and phone extension numbers on the first page, which was obviously all the people that worked there. The rest of the pages contained a lot of names and phone numbers that meant nothing to us, but obviously did to Thaxted. Sam photographed every page. My book was much thicker, also A4 in size and was just over forty pages in length, with five properties on each page. The pages had the name of the relevant country, the name and exact location of a property, a picture of the outside of the property, and what was described as the guide price. There were also various bits of information on the last few pages which I didn't bother to read. But as instructed, I dutifully photographed everything. We finished and I turned off the light after noting where the door handle was. We waited a full minute with our eyes shut, and then opened the door and went back into Naomi's office. I closed the shower room door behind me.

'I've finished here,' said Martin. 'I've copied everything on to a portable hard drive I brought with me and I'll leave that with you when we get back to the hotel. Now, have you any idea where the accounts department is?'

'Not a clue I'm afraid,' said Sam. 'We‘ve only been in Naomi's office, the DVD screening room and reception downstairs.'

'OK, in that case let's go hunting. Follow me and don't open any doors until I say so.'

'Message received and definitely understood,' I replied.

We eventually found the accounts office on the top floor, and after a brief discussion it was decided to copy everything from all three computers onto portable hard drives, and while Martin was occupied with that, I photographed all the cheque stubs from two used chequebooks along with another list of names and phone numbers. We took a few minutes trying to think if we could obtain anything else while we were in the building, and decided we had everything we needed. Then we left the building the same way we had come, with Martin putting everything back exactly where it had come from. He closed the window behind him, locked it from the outside, and then finally turned the alarm back on with his remote device. We eventually got back to the hotel around three o'clock, went to our room and after a celebratory drink, headed to bed.

Chapter Twenty-Two

I got up bright and early at eight o'clock feeling remarkably fresh and wide awake. Sadly I couldn't say the same for Sam. I thought she was joking at first, but then she assured me she wasn't. She'd got food poisoning for real. I telephoned Naomi to let her know and despite my saying not to bother, she insisted on coming to our hotel to wish Sam a speedy recovery. I eventually gave in and Naomi saw Sam in the flesh so to speak, and there was no doubt in her mind. Sam had got food poisoning.

'It was that awful burger and chips from the market stall last night,' I said. 'We should have eaten in the hotel again and never have gone there.'

'Funnily enough,' said Naomi, 'Casandra and her boyfriend were in the market last night listening to the local reggae band, and she said she saw you both with some guy she didn't recognise, and was going to warn you about the dodgy food you occasionally get from some of the stalls, but she didn't like to butt in as you were with company.'

'Oh I wish she had done,' said Sam as she quickly launched herself off the sofa and rushed for the bathroom where she was violently sick again. I knew it—we had been followed. Casandra being in the market at the same time as us? That was definitely no coincidence.

'Poor Sam,' said Naomi, 'she's definitely in no fit state to fly. By the way, it's not really important Michael but just out of interest—the guy you were with last night? I trust it was another prospective client for me who I'm sure you told all about Thaxted?'

'Well yes, your name did come up in passing, but sadly I don't think he'll be buying any of your properties,' I said. 'We met him by chance here in the hotel over a cup of tea yesterday afternoon and got chatting. I gather he's some kind of mechanical and hydraulics engineer who works mainly for the oil industry, and apparently he's here to do some technical work on a broken crane in the docks.'

Sam slowly walked back into the lounge from the bathroom and simply collapsed in a heap on the sofa moaning quietly in the background. Naomi wished Sam better soon and then bade us farewell with me promising that I would get in touch with her to rearrange our trip to Venice as soon as Sam was feeling up to flying and back on her feet.

No sooner had I shut the door on Naomi than Sam scared the life out of me when she jumped off the sofa and rapidly headed for our bedroom.

'Come on you,' she said, 'book us on the next flight out of here while I do the packing.'

'What the hell happened to your dreadful food poisoning?' I asked.

'Oh really Michael—after all these months, and you still can't tell when I'm faking it?' she said with a glint in her eye and a really big grin on her lips. We were packed in ten minutes flat, while also including the four portable hard drives that Martin had left with us, and which we'd kept in our room safe overnight. We threw everything in the car and drove on minor roads to the airport, as the main road would have taken us straight past Thaxted's building, and we didn't want to risk being seen. We caught a ten-thirty flight to Miami, and then having decided to stay overnight, we booked a couple of business class seats on the early morning British Airways flight to London. Well, why not I reasoned? Interpol were paying!

We'd also decided that as we were going to be in London anyway, it made perfect sense to call in at Greenwich and bring Stephen and Paul up to date, assuming they would be there. As soon as we got to London, I rang Stephen, and we agreed to meet in his office at ten o'clock the following morning. I also telephoned Kurt and thanked him for introducing us to the slightly scary and interestingly intriguing world of Martin Smith. Kurt said Martin had already been in touch and given him a full report on all that had happened. Kurt suggested that if possible, we should give the hard drives to Stephen straight away, and then he could download everything overnight. Stephen would also send copies to both Kurt and Helena as their might be information on De Beers's people Kurt may know of, or on Dutch stone cutters that Helena might recognise. So we got a train from the airport to Greenwich, dropped the hard discs off with Paul who said he would get their tech team on it straight away. We confirmed out meeting for ten o'clock the following morning, left the police station and checked into the new five star InterContinental hotel next to the O2 arena just down the road in Greenwich. As I said before—Interpol were paying!

The following morning we arrived at the police station and were taken straight to the conference room. Stephen and Paul were waiting for us along with Detective Sergeant Richard Thorpe, one of their tech guys.

'Good morning to both of you on this bright and sunny day!' exclaimed Stephen in what can only be described as a very cheery voice.

'What are you on about, Stephen?' asked Sam. 'It's extremely wet and foggy outside.'

'Ah, but it's sunny in my heart today,' he replied. 'You know the information you two obtained on your little Caribbean holiday has cheered me up no end.'

'I feel I should point out Superintendent dearest,' said Sam, 'that our Caribbean holiday as you so disingenuously call it was fraught with danger throughout, and we both risked life and limb getting you that information.'

'Yes, said Paul. 'I heard all about your fake food poisoning. You do realise Sam that if something is fake it is not the real thing, and therefore you were not actually ill?'

'I think Sam was referring to our highly dangerous exploratory meeting with Naomi Gardiner,' I said, 'where I should point out we had to be on our guard with every word we spoke as I dread to think what she would have done if we'd dropped ourselves in it. I'm sure they must have had trained thugs or assassins on hand. Then we were followed as if we were criminals by Casandra Dufreine, who is obviously a criminal of some sort, and we had to be very careful in everything we did with her tailing us, and then of course there was the minor matter of the pair of us breaking in to Thaxted's highly guarded headquarters in the dead of night.'

'Yes, true, but you did have Martin to hold your hand,' laughed Paul.

'Enough of this frivolity,' said Stephen. 'Seriously you two, well done. Kurt and Helena will be joining us for a conference call in about fifteen minutes, but I've asked Richard here, who happens to be our chief tech guy, to fill you in on everything he's managed to pull of the hard drives and the photographs you supplied. Richard—over to you.'

'Good morning Sam, good morning Michael. It's nice to meet you both having heard so much about you both from Paul.'

'Oh for goodness sake get on with it Richard,' said Stephen, 'we haven't got all day!'

'Yes, fine, OK. Well, firstly you'll be pleased to know we have now got an address for Derek and Sandra Simpson, and you were right, it's in the Spanish town of Mijas.

Naomi's computer threw up a host of postal addresses, email addresses and mobile phone numbers. Reading between the lines of some of the emails which are obviously using some sort of innocent looking messages about various Thaxted properties, it looks as if the procedure they follow is for Francois Viljoen in Cape Town to text the details of the next shipment of uncut stones potentially worth stealing to Caroline Chambers using a single use burner phone. We know this because we came across several mobile phone numbers that no longer exist, but the service providers have co-operated with Interpol and have given us what details they had, although I'm afraid nothing would stand up in court. Caroline then gives the information to Dominic St Clair, using another burner phone which she then ditches. As they both live in Mijas, we assume St Clair then passes the information to Derek Simpson face to face, that way ensuring that there is no electronic or paper trail. We have nothing in writing and no texts as such, but thanks to the service providers we can state categorically that Viljoen texts Caroline Chambers via burner phones that are used for just one text and then binned, and then three minutes later, Caroline Chambers sends a text to St Clair using another mobile which is then binned immediately after. We can trace this pattern having happened at least three times over the last two months, including your friend Mr Tisbury's package.'

'You say none of this will stand up in court?' I asked.

'No it won't,' confirmed Stephen. 'Part of the problem we're facing here is the sheer amount of different countries involved in all this, and which if any country, can claim jurisdiction? We are talking about South Africa, the UK, Spain, Portugal, The Bahamas, The Netherlands and we suspect Italy and the United Arab Emirates as well. For all we know at this stage there could be another twenty countries involved.'

'But surely that's where Interpol come in?' I asked.

'You'd think so, wouldn't you?' said Stephen 'But most police forces around the world only co-operate with Interpol under sufferance. They would much prefer to keep something like this under their own jurisdiction, so that they get the glory, and solving big cases like this one is turning out to be, gives them more clout when they go to their respective governments to ask for more funding. I'm afraid it's the same everywhere in the world—including here in the UK.'

'So what else have we found out?' asked Sam

'Well,' replied Stephen. 'Richard here is pretty sure there is some sort of clearing house for want of a better word in Italy. Thaxted seem to have a massive amount of communication with Venice, and it's a pity in a way that you didn't get there, but at least we can now give you a lot more information for your next trip.'

'Which is when?' I asked

'Well first,' said Stephen, 'we'd like you both to go over and meet with Helena in Amsterdam, later this week if possible, and check out a particular diamond cutter we suspect is heavily involved—a guy named Hannes de Jaeger who Helena already suspected.'

'De Jaeger knows who Helena is and what she does,' said Richard, 'and like most criminals, he knows who all the cops are, but you two would be total unknowns.'

'After you've found out what we need to know in Amsterdam,' said Stephen taking over again, 'we'd like you to visit Venice for a week or so, with Helena, and then if you're happy to do so, we'd then like the three of you to go on to Dubai, where Kurt will meet up with you. Assuming that is that you're both still happy to continue in your roles as official police consultants and investigators—but be warned, the more involved you get in all of this the more dangerous it is likely to become.'

'No problem,' I replied. 'I know I speak for both of us when I say we're determined to see this through to the end. And talking of danger—any sign of that murdering scum Freddie Drayton at Simpson's villa, or anywhere else for that matter?'

'We have no idea who is living in the villa I'm afraid. We've looked at the place using Google Earth, but that hasn't really been much help. No, I'm afraid we only have his address. We also searched via Interpol's files, but there is no mention of the name Freddie Drayton anywhere in the world in the last eight years. We suspect he is based in Mijas as well, but probably under a false identity. Spain is full of ex criminals, including, I'm sure, plenty of forgers who could have provided him with a false identity.' I sat quietly for a minute or two with an interesting thought going through my mind.

'I don't know if this idea would work,' I said slowly, 'but a few months ago I wanted to get some nice aerial footage of the villa I live in to email to some friends of mine, and so I treated myself to a really good drone. You know, one of these helicopter type things with four propellers—it looks like a kid's toy, but they work really well. Anyway, I was wondering, could Richard here fit it out with a good quality video camera armed with a really powerful telescopic lens, and then I could fly it high over Simpson's villa and hopefully see who lives there?'

'That could work, Superintendent,' jumped in Richard. 'I've got the ideal video camera and recording equipment in the tech department, plus we've got an excellent drone of our own which I could learn to fly if Michael and Sam have to go to Holland, Venice and Dubai'

'Nice try, Richard,' said Stephen, 'but you're needed here. Answer me honestly Michael, how well can you fly this drone of yours?'

'Certainly well enough to get some decent film, particularly if I flew just the drone and Sam operated the camera by remote control. We'd need to fly it quite high of course so that they didn't hear the noise of the drone, and therefore we'd need really good telephoto facilities for getting close ups.'

'Can I suggest a quick day trip to Mijas for our intrepid heroes,' suggested Paul, 'and then head to Venice at the weekend. That gives Richard and his team plenty of time to finish pulling all the information off of the hard drives. We could all meet back here on Friday say, organise another conference call where we can all get an update.'

'That's fine with me,' I said, 'but Sam still has a medical practice to run, and I don't want this to cost her, her career.'

'I'd already thought about that,' said Sam, 'and I emailed an old college friend of mine, Dr Sylvester McClain yesterday, and asked him if he could fly out and fill in for me as a locum for a few weeks. We studied together at medical school and he's now running a practice in Edinburgh, but he's got five other GP's under him, so he is quite able to make himself available and he is more than happy to help.'

'Fantastic,' said Stephen. 'In that case then, can I suggest Michael that you practice flying Richard's drone once he's fitted the video camera on it, and assuming you can master it in time, you and Sam fly out to Málaga first thing in the morning, get your filming done over the Simpson's villa, and then fly back later the same day?'

After our conference call with Kurt and Helena, Sam and I joined Richard who had already fitted the camera, and we went outside for a test run. Fortunately Richard's drone, although a professional model was virtually identical to my own, and after ten minutes I felt confident enough to proclaim I was now an official police drone pilot. I don't think the police saw it quite like that, but it made me happy. Sam got some detailed lessons on operating the video camera via the remote control, and we both had lessons in how to set everything up and get everything working. I was also given a dedicated mobile phone that only had one number on it, and that went straight through to Richard if we needed any technical help. Sam and I then visited the local launderette and got all our clothes freshly laundered at Interpol's expense. Then we returned to the police station where Paul had by then, booked us the early morning flight to Malaga, hired a car for us and also booked us a room at the Hilton at Gatwick Airport. The drone, complete with its camera, remote control and two TV monitors was already sealed in two heavy duty protective flight cases, covered in "handle with care" and "do not touch" stickers, and booked in with return flights on a top cargo airline as official police equipment to be delivered to Málaga airport overnight. It would be waiting for us when we arrived.

Chapter Twenty-Three

We duly arrived at Málaga at 8:45 am with just our hand luggage, and after presenting all the relevant paperwork, we picked up the two flight cases, loaded it all into the hire car, a Hyundai 4 x 4, and then headed for Mijas. It was a glorious day with no wind—ideal for flying the drone.

'Where do we set up, Michael?' Sam asked. 'I guess we need to be above the villa, but not be seen by anybody else?'

'Exactly,' I replied. 'Let's look for a spot near that garden looking out to sea. I'm pretty sure there are loads of bushes where we can set up and be pretty hidden.'

We'd parked the 4 x 4 Paul had hired for us in the car park nearest the old bull ring and walked up through the town carrying a flight case each to the garden area we'd discussed. It was only nine-thirty and Mijas was still mostly asleep. Nothing much happens until ten o'clock in this part of the world when the shops open, and so we had an opportunity to find the perfect spot without being watched. When we were a hundred percent sure nobody was around and watching us, we climbed over the wall, taking all the equipment with us, and then walked to the right, away from the garden for about 50 yards where we managed to find a secluded area behind some large bushes from where we could set up, being totally hidden from anyone in the garden above us by the bushes and several trees. From our secret hidey hole, we could still see the various villas in the area where Derek Simpson had his retreat. We set up the equipment and I sent up the drone getting it well away from us as soon as possible. According to Richard the drone could fly for over an hour before crashing to the ground, but he suggested we only do forty five minute flights before bringing it down for battery changes. I was amazed how quiet it was compared to my own drone, but then again this was a police surveillance drone and lack of noise was an essential part of its design. I flew it around for five minutes getting a feel for the controls while Sam was watching the camera feed on her large monitor. The colour picture she was seeing was identical to the smaller black and white picture I was receiving on the remote control's monitor, but that was quite adequate for my needs. Looking across at Sam's large colour monitor I now understood why Richard had insisted on us taking the two large monitors, the spare being just in case one of them didn't work for some unknown reason. The large monitor for Sam was making her job ten times easier.

'OK, I guess it's time to watch the Simpsons,' I said.

'No,' said Sam, 'we haven't got time to go and watch silly cartoons on the television. Sorry Michael, I've been looking for an opportunity to say something like that for ages.' I just smiled back.

'Here we go,' I said and headed the drone east towards the villa we wanted to observe.

'I can't hear it at all, Sam,' I said, 'but to be on the safe side I'm going to take it even higher, so you may need to increase the zoom.'

'No problem,' replied Sam. 'The camera on this thing is amazing.' I took the drone another hundred feet up and brought it over Derek Simpson's villa. Sam had a large seventeen-inch full colour monitor in front of her, which gave her excellent high definition pictures, and I had a smaller seven inch version attached to the remote control I was using to fly the drone. We were both watching the same input from the camera.

'That's the one!' I exclaimed, 'and there are people sitting in the garden having breakfast. Can you zoom in a bit tighter Sam so that we can see who they are?' Sam did just that until the breakfast table was virtually filling the screen.

'The guy in the purple tee shirt and white shorts is Derek Simpson,' said Sam, 'and that's the lovely Sandra sitting opposite him.'

'And if I'm not mistaken,' I said excitedly, 'the other guy is the elusive Freddie Drayton.'

'You're right,' said Sam as she pulled back on the remote to give us a wider picture.

'I'd recognise him anywhere,' I said.

'Oh, hold on!' exclaimed Sam, 'two more for breakfast by the look of it.'

'That's Jimmy Priestly in the jeans and the unmistakable shape of muscle man Alex Donovan. Good God!' I exclaimed. 'Do you think they all live together?' I asked Sam.

'Well the house is certainly big enough,' she said while pulling the camera lens even further back. 'Look Michael, there's a smaller annexe-type building over to the side of the property, and those two arrived from that direction. My bet is that Drayton, Priestly and Donavan all share the annexe so that Simpson has them on hand and at his beck and call anytime he wants them.'

'That wouldn't surprise me at all,' I said. 'I'm going to fly this thing to the other side of the property where I noticed some cars parked at the front. Let's see if we can get close enough to get registration plates. I'm sure Interpol can get us more details from who each of the cars are registered to.'

I managed to hover the drone right over the cars, but from its position above we could only see the roof of each car, and not the registration plates.

'Sam, can you alter the angle of the camera if I fly a bit lower and a bit further away to give you room. Try if you can to zoom in and get all three registration plates and I'll try and manoeuvre it to a suitable angle?'

I flew the drone further away from the front of the villa, and then dropped it lower, and I was pleased to see Sam had zoomed in on the three cars. Two were parked neatly facing out, and one was parked at a slight angle and facing in towards the house. My immediate thought was that the two parked facing out were Derek's and Sandra's, and the other one was a visitor's car. Perhaps Freddie Drayton didn't live there after all and had only popped over for breakfast? Anyway, we'd now got video of the registration plates, so I took the drone away from their villa, lifted it up a hundred feet and completed several passes over the house, all at a height where I could guarantee the drone wouldn't be seen or heard, and Sam filmed everything at different zoom levels on each pass. There was a sudden "ding" sound from Sam's mobile phone.

'Michael, the drones been flying for forty minutes now, we need to bring it back and get it safely on the ground. I put a forty minute stop watch on my mobile when the drone took off. I thought it safest.'

'Well done!' I exclaimed. 'Idiot that I am I should have thought of that, but didn't.'

I took the drone up even higher and flew it back past us for about half a mile, and once it was well past our position, I brought it down lower to just above tree level and then carefully flew it back to our position. Once it was back on the ground, Sam said, 'What was all that about? Why the fly past?'

'Just in case anyone was watching the drone. We're pretty sure no-one at the villa would have seen it, but what if Dominic was in his garden and saw it for example. It's unlikely as his villa is in the middle of town and doesn't overlook Derek Simpson's, but just to be on the safe side, I want anyone who may have seen it in the air to think it came from somewhere other than here, which should give us time to get back to the car and drive away from here.'

'Good thinking, Batman,' laughed Sam. 'In that case let's pack away everything as soon as possible and get the hell out of here.'

We hastily did just that. Sam neatly packed everything into their flight cases, including the two portable hard drives that now contained everything we'd filmed. We walked back to the car, put everything in the boot and headed out of Mijas and back to Málaga. Once we'd got back to the seafront we took a room in a hotel, and I texted Richard who gave me instructions on how to wire in the two hard drives to my laptop, and then he took over the operation of everything by remote control. Don't ask me how he did it or how it works, I haven't a clue, but I got a text from Richard about 40 minutes later saying he'd received everything. Our flight wasn't for another five hours, so we passed some of the time away in the area outside our hotel on the seafront where we could see our parked car at all times. We hadn't eaten since we arrived in Spain, so we thought we'd indulge ourselves by having a pot of tea and two much needed full English breakfasts.

Once we'd finished our leisurely breakfasts, we headed back to the airport, checked the flight cases back in for their return flight with the cargo company Paul had used, and then we eventually flew back to Gatwick ourselves. We stayed overnight in the same hotel and tipped up at Greenwich police station at ten o'clock the following morning. We asked for Stephen, but were told he was out giving evidence in court and was due back later, so Paul came out and took us into the conference room for a quick debrief.

'How did it go?' he asked.

'Pretty well,' I replied. 'I think we got all the film we could, and as a bonus we also managed to film the registration plates of three cars parked in the front of the villa. We assume you can trace who owns them from the registration plates even though they are Spanish?'

'We're pretty sure we can guess which car belongs to which person anyway, just by their makes and models,' said Sam. 'For example, one of the cars is a lovely maroon Bentley Continental convertible which we reckon has got to be Derek Simpson's, and parked next to it was a pale blue BMW M3 convertible. I reckon that has to be Sandra Simpsons as I can't imagine any man buying a pale blue car.

'Makes sense,' agreed Paul.

'The third car,' continued Sam, 'was a bright red Porsche 911 turbo, which we reckon belongs to Freddie Drayton who we saw there, but we think he was just visiting them for breakfast and a chat.'

'Obviously the car thing is all guesswork,' I said, 'but hopefully you can get registration information through Interpol.'

'Oh no problem,' said Paul. 'Richard has downloaded all the film you took and he has been going over it ever since. Stephen should be back from court any minute and then we'll all watch it together and decide what we do next and where we go from there.'

Stephen was indeed back from court ten minutes later, and he had a few phone calls to make before meeting with us, but fifteen minutes later Sam, Stephen, Paul, Richard and I all sat down in the conference room to watch our Stephen Spielberg-like efforts. Paul had as usual ordered tea and biscuits. We sat and watched the film for about thirty minutes, which was the length of the useful bits.

'I sent the registration numbers to Interpol,' said Paul, 'and they have confirmed your guesses about the Bentley and the BMW. They are registered to Derek and Sandra Simpson in their real names, and they obviously are quite happy that people know who they are.'

'Of course they are,' moaned Stephen. 'The police in numerous countries have been after them for fifteen years to my knowledge, and nobody anywhere has ever been able to prove a thing against them—not even a bloody traffic ticket. They think they're untouchable, but I think this time round we may just get them.'

'As for the Porsche 911, there's no link to Freddie Drayton what-so-ever. The car is registered to a guy named Andrew Roman Chichalo. From what I've been able to find out, he's a Ukrainian who apparently moved to Europe with his parents when he was about 3 years old, but then there's no record on file of him anywhere after that, until he turned up in Spain about ten years ago. There is nothing I can see to connect this guy to the elusive Freddie Drayton.'

'Oh brilliant!' I said, 'he's absolutely bloody brilliant—priceless even.'

'What is it?' asked Stephen. 'You obviously know something we don't.'

'Bear with me,' I began. 'A couple of years ago I was researching a new travel book for my publishers on the locations of various crimes in Russia, and I came across that name. As I remember it, the rough gist is that in October 1936, a boy was born in the small town of Yabluchne in the Ukraine. Fifty-six years later in April 1992 he was tried in Rostov, Russia and sentenced to death for the murders of 52 men, women and children, although he claimed to have actually murdered 57 people. He mutilated all his victims and usually cut and slashed their throats with a knife. He was known throughout his trial by several nicknames including the Red Ripper, the Rostov Ripper and the Butcher of Rostov, but his real name however was Andrei Romanovich Chikatilo. I believe our Mr Andrew Roman Chichalo is in fact Freddie Drayton who has named himself after one of the world's most notorious serial killers, who also had a trademark of slashing his victim's throats with a knife.'

'Urgh, that's just sick,' said Sam.

'I agree,' said Paul, 'but Freddie Drayton is one hell of a sick individual.'

'I don't know about you,' I said, 'but for me that is enough to confirm that Andrew Roman Chichalo and Freddie Drayton are one and the same person.'

'Amazing!' exclaimed Stephen. 'Freddie Drayton has re-named himself after a killer he sees as some kind of hero, a bloody Russian serial killer?'

'Well Ukrainian actually,' I corrected, 'but yes, it has to be him. There are too many coincidences for it not to be Freddie Drayton, including the simple fact of his car being parked in Derek Simpson's villa yesterday morning.'

'OK,' said Stephen. 'Moving on. Are you two still happy to stick with our original plan and visit Amsterdam to see what you can find out about Hannes de Jaeger,' said Stephen, 'and then move on to Venice for a week or so with Helena, and then the three of you to go on to Dubai, where Kurt will meet up with you and fill you in on what's needed there? I'm very conscious that you've hardly stopped travelling round the world for the last few weeks and you must be bloody exhausted.'

'As our cockney friends would say,' said Sam, 'totally cream-crackered.' Paul and Richard both looked perplexed.

'Cream-crackered is cockney rhyming slang for knackered,' I explained as light dawned on their faces. 'Good grief,' I continued, 'I have to fly from Portugal to explain cockney rhyming slang to two Londoners. The world's gone mad.'

'I'm not a Londoner,' said Paul 'I was born and grew up in Cambridge. I know nothing about cockney rhyming slang!'

'Same here,' said Richard. 'I grew up on a small farm in Norfolk, and then got my Masters at Oxford. How would I know anything about cockney rhyming slang?'

'But surely you would know what I meant if I said my trouble and strife fell down the apples and pears?' I appealed.

'Not a clue,' said Paul.

'That means his wife, as in trouble and strife, fell down the stairs, as in apples and pears,' smiled Stephen, obviously very pleased with himself.

'Of all the people Superintendent, I would never put you down as the one policeman in this room that knew cockney rhyming slang,' said Sam, equally amazed.

'Ah, well not being cash and carried and living on me Jack Jones, meant I could put a Tom, Dick and Harry of phrases on the Henry Moore of the Kermit, and Captain Cook up something new whenever I had an Eartha Kitt.'

‘Stephen,’ I said. ‘I have to admit, you have without doubt gone up in my estimation a million fold. You are truly to be admired.’

‘What the hell did the boss just say?’ asked Richard.

‘An approximate translation,’ I replied, ‘would be “Not being married and living on my own enabled me to hang a dictionary of cockney phrases on the door of the toilet, and look up new phrases whenever I was having a shit”.’

‘Bloody hell,’ replied Richard, ‘learning Latin at Oxford was so much easier.’

Sam and I flew back to the Algarve and spent a few days recovering, and then armed with two fairly full suitcases of clothes, we headed to Faro airport yet again where we boarded Transavia flight number 5356 to Amsterdam which leaves Faro at 7 pm every night. We landed at Amsterdam’s Schiphol Airport where we were met by Helena who greeted us like long lost friends and took us back to her apartment. She’d suggested we stay with her rather than book into a hotel so that we could chat anytime. After settling in to her very nice modern apartment, we all collapsed in very comfy armchairs with a bottle of South African Merlot, especially bought for the occasion by Helena, and we filled her in on everything we’d done since leaving her in Cape Town. At one in the morning, we decided it was time to call it a day, and Sam and I went to bed.

Chapter Twenty-Four

The following morning the three of us sat and chatted over a typical continental breakfast of rolls, cheese and cold meats, with lots of coffee, although I made myself a mug of tea. We'd brought Helena up to date the previous night and it was now time to turn our attention to Mr Hannes de Jaeger—Amsterdam's finest Diamond Cutter & Polisher.

'We have to be very careful with this guy,' said Helena. 'He's very clever and very suspicious of anyone new. He knows me and all the police in Amsterdam; moreover, he keeps himself very much to himself.'

'What exactly is it you want us to do, and what information do you want us to try and get from him?' Sam asked.

'Well, in all honesty, we know very little, and can prove even less. We think he works for Derek Simpson, but we don't know for sure, and it would help us tremendously if you could find out if he does. You can't search anywhere, or leave any fingerprints. Don't wear gloves—it will look too suspicious, but if you do manage to get inside, don't touch anything. I'm afraid you'll just have to find out what you can through conversation alone.'

'And how the hell do we do that?' I asked.

'Well my thinking was that you could tell him you're looking for a good cutter and polisher for a not strictly kosher job, and his name was given to you by Ronnie da Silva.'

The canal in Amsterdam where Hannes de Jaeger lives

The canal in Amsterdam where Helena lives

The diamond cutting and polishing work of Hannes de Jaeger

One of Amsterdam's many sight seeing boats

'Surely the first thing he'll do is telephone this Ronnie da Silva guy to check us out?'

'He can't. Ronnie da Silva is dead. He was stabbed and pushed into a canal last month.'

'God! Any idea who did it?' asked Sam.

'Yes,' replied Helena, 'it was a local gang thing, and the Amsterdam police arrested the killer two days after the murder. He's currently on remand in Bijlmerbajes. That's the prison in Amsterdam near Spaklerweg Metro Station.'

'So the idea,' I said, 'is we tell him we've got a lucrative job for him, offer him a decent financial incentive and hope he tells us something linking him to Derek Simpson?'

'Yes,' replied Helena. 'That's basically it. Not very scientific I know, but sometimes the simplest of plans work!' Helena gave us his address and directions, and we left her apartment mid-morning heading for the red light district, which is where Hannes de Jaeger lived and worked. We decided to walk as it gave us time to discuss our approach, and the twenty minute stroll should have been very pleasant, but our minds were on other things than how scenic our journey was. We arrived at the big wooden front door which was pretty old looking and quite tatty, and I rang the doorbell. There was a speaker on the wall next to the door, but there was no name by either the bell or the speaker. The speaker spoke to me in a fairly gruff voice.

'Ja.'

'Oh good morning. Do you speak English by any chance?' I asked.

'Yes', came the same gruff voice. 'Who are you and what do you want?'

'I'm from England and I'm looking to speak with a Mr Hannes de Jaeger. I was sent here and given this address by

Ronnie da Silva.' I replied, hoping the use of his name might elicit a positive response. There was a long silence that seemed to last forever, and then the door speaker suddenly buzzed and the lock clicked. Sam and I looked at each other as Sam indicated a CCTV camera high above the window to our right which was pointing directly at us. I sort of waved at the camera and pushed the door open. We entered a very dark and dinghy hallway with nothing other than an equally dark and dinghy flight of stairs in front of us. The place looked incredibly run down, dirty, smelly and incredibly scruffy, hardly the location of Amsterdam's finest diamond cutter & polisher, but then I guess that's what he wanted visitors and the police to think. I turned to close the front door behind us, but it shut automatically on its own, and as it did so, I noticed that both the door and the door frame were lined with what looked like heavy grade steel sheet. We went up the stairs and I noticed there was another CCTV camera in the top corner, also pointing directly at us. I tentatively knocked on the door facing us.

The door slowly opened, and we were faced with a small man, probably about five foot four in height, but quite rotund and in his early sixties I estimated. He was standing in a small, filthy looking hallway about five-foot square, with another closed door hiding the room behind him.

'Good morning,' I started. 'Mr de Jaeger I presume. My name is David Fanshaw, and this is my wife Gloria.' We'd decided to stop using our real names as Helena pointed out, too many people who know each other might mention in passing having met a Michael and Sam and they just might start putting two and two together. De Jaeger still didn't invite us in.

'I repeat, what do you want?'

'As I said, your name was given to us by Ronnie da Silva who said you would be the best man to help us with a cutting job that wasn't one hundred percent kosher, if you see what I mean?'

'I do, and when did Mr da Silva recommend me may I ask?' asked de Jaeger.

'Oh, that would have been about six or seven weeks ago.' I replied 'I've been trying to get hold of him for the last week or so, but he's not answering his mobile.'

'Mmm,' mused de Jaeger. 'Let me check you have the right number?' he said and held out his hand for my mobile. Fortunately Helena, who knew this guy quite well and just how cautious he was, had put Ronnie da Silva's correct mobile number into my phone. So having brought up the number on to the screen I happily handed over my phone.

'I'm sure it's the right number,' I said, 'as he and I have spoken on it several times. I can only assume he's not able to answer for some reason.'

'That's because Ronnie da Silva is dead,' said De Jaeger, 'you better come in.'

We entered the apartment through the second door. The view that greeted us was a complete contrast to what we had seen outside. It was an incredibly large, very bright and beautifully furnished apartment. Cream and white walls, white leather sofas, stainless steel everywhere with the only colour in the room being provided by rich maroon curtains and cushions. De Jaeger had obviously spent a lot of his ill-gotten gains on the apartment, and it showed.

'In my line of work I have to be extremely careful, hence the scruffy stairs and the dirty hallway. Nobody who doesn't know me has a clue what goes on in here,' he said.

Well Sam and I knew what went on, as did the Amsterdam police and Interpol, but we weren't about to tell him that.

'Please sit down and tell me exactly what you want.'

'Well,' I began. You may have noticed, I begin of lot of my sentences with a "well" followed by a pause. It gives me time to think. 'Gloria and I have recently come into possession of a quantity of uncut diamonds,' I continued. 'We can't however do much with them until they have been cut, polished and mounted. I met Ronnie in an East End pub in London a few weeks ago, and we'd both had a few drinks and got chatting. One thing led to another, I mentioned my problem and he suggested you might be able to help me.'

'Can I ask how you came to acquire the stones, Mr Fanshaw?'

'Ah, well, there was a night time break in at a Hatton Garden jewellers a couple of months ago, and although I wasn't involved directly with the break in, I did pass some information on to the people who did the job about the alarm and the various security codes. That's what I do for a living—I'm a security guard. Anyway, they gave me quite a few of the uncut stones as my share for getting them the information they needed.'

De Jaeger was obviously not very impressed with my credentials.

'Look, I'm sorry, Mr Fanshaw, I appreciate this is a one-off job, but as much as I would love to help you, I'm afraid I can't. I am fully committed with work for the next few months, and I also have several long term projects booked with the same client who I am under contract to.'

'Surely they would understand if you explained?'

'I'm afraid the only thing my client understands is getting her own way, and besides, there is this little thing called client confidentiality. I only agreed to talk to you because Ronnie had mentioned my name. I liked Ronnie and he and I got on very well, but he was killed recently, and I cannot risk getting involved. I'm sorry to say this, but to be perfectly frank with you Mr Fanshaw, you have been far too relaxed about talking to a total stranger about what you do. You don't know me at all, and yet you've just told me about your involvement in a robbery. I'm sorry, but it's the way it has to be in this business—I would never tell you anything about my clients, and likewise—I will never mention our conversation to them.'

'I see.' I paused as if deep in thought. 'Look, could you perhaps just help us in the evenings or something without saying anything to these people you have a contract with.'

'No, I'm sorry, Mr Fanshaw, my decision is final, and I really can't help you. God, if Heinrich found out I was doing work on the side she'd have my balls cut off and included as part of her next necklace. Look, I'm sorry, but I have already said far too much. Please forget completely about me and my address, and I promise, I will totally forget about you. I assume you are both intelligent enough to understand the consequences should you fail to keep quiet about our meeting. Goodbye, Mr and Mrs Fanshaw.'

De Jaeger stood up, and that was obviously the end of our very brief conversation. He then very firmly ushered us out of his front door.

'Please remember,' he said, 'you've never seen me nor heard of me, nor I of you. Goodbye to you both.'

Hannes de Jaeger slammed the door shut behind us and we gingerly walked down the stairs and out of the house. We slowly walked along the side of the canal returning to Helena's, feeling quite dejected in that we seemed to have achieved absolutely nothing. I turned to speak to Sam and suddenly realised that she wasn't walking beside me anymore. She'd stopped a couple of paces back and was staring down at the water in the canal.

'I've got it!' she suddenly exclaimed quite excitedly.

'Got what?' I queried.

'Tell me,' she asked, 'what are Sandra Simpson's initials?'

'SS of course,' I replied, 'so what?'

'And who was the head of the SS?' Sam asked.

We both answered the question aloud in unison, having both understood its meaning.

'Heinrich Himmler!'

'Sandra Simpson is Heinrich, and from the way De Jaeger was speaking, that means she's the boss!' exclaimed Sam, 'not Derek. He said she would turn his balls into a necklace, and he was bloody terrified of her. I'm positive that means Sandra Simpson runs the show.'

We hugged each other, had a quick kiss and then set off back to Helena's in a much lighter frame of mind. When we got back we filled her in on the details of our conversation, and she completely concurred with our conclusions. Helena then sent what we'd learnt off to Stephen and Kurt in an encrypted email, and the three of us ate an evening meal together.

It was during the meal that I had my "great idea", although at that stage I kept my thoughts to myself until I'd slept on them.

Chapter Twenty-Five

The following morning I offered to cook the three of us that good old English staple "The Full English", after which I said I wanted to outline my great idea.

'OK then Einstein, startle us with your stunningly brilliant plan,' began Sam.

'Well,' I said. 'We can't arrest the Simpsons at the moment as we have no proof that they've done anything illegal. We have no concrete evidence that links them to any specific crime—at least nothing which will stand up in court—and everything we do have against them is purely circumstantial. Sam and I are both British and have no authority in any country, including the UK, and our perpetrators are safely holed up in Spain—where as far as we know they've committed no crimes. To make matters worse, although Spain officially has an extradition treaty with the UK, we can't prove they've done anything illegal, and even if we could, by the time extradition proceedings reached the Spanish courts we'd all be old age pensioners or dead.

'So what's your great idea?' asked Helena.

'Smoke them out. Present them with something so tempting that they simply couldn't turn it down, also we'd have to set it up in the Algarve so that they felt they could safely high tail it back to Spain in less than an hour. We'd need to involve the GNR, Interpol, De Beers, and the UK police as our suspects are all British citizens, and if they're all involved in the planning and we're all there waiting for them, then we should be able to catch them in the act. Once we've got them for one crime, we can then hit them with everything else we've got.'

'Well I like it,' smiled Sam. 'What do you think Helena?'

'I like it as well. Tell me Michael—what exactly did you mean by "present them with something so tempting they simply couldn't turn it down?"'

'Oh...Um—well I had nothing specific in mind—but just say for example, De Beers accidentally let it slip to Francois Viljoen that a delivery of 30 million pounds worth of uncut diamonds was being sent to the Algarve, and this time they were being carried by a single courier so as not to draw attention, but unfortunately that meant he will have to keep the stones with him overnight in his hotel room. We don't actually have to have 30 million quid's worth—just as long as the Simpsons believe we do. I'm sure De Beers would co-operate if we went straight to the top man and explained what we believe has been going on. We could set the trap and hopefully they'd walk into it.'

'We'd have to be very careful,' said Helena, 'that what we do is legal, and couldn't be classed as entrapment, but I could work that out with Kurt and Superintendent Colshaw.'

'OK ladies, well in that case can I suggest we telephone Stephen in London and see if we can arrange a get together of all the interested parties. As I said, I think we need to involve the UK Police, Interpol, The Portuguese Police and De Beers, and as "the sting" for want of a better word is going to take place on Portuguese soil I suggest we all meet in the Algarve.'

'I'll organise three plane tickets to Faro for later today if possible.' said Helena.

True to her word—three hours later we boarded a flight from Schiphol to Faro.

While Helena had been booking our plane tickets, I'd had a lengthy chat with Stephen, brought him up to date with what we'd learnt in the Netherlands and then outlined our idea. Stephen was on board straight away and he made a few international phone calls. The long and the short of it was that we'd all be meeting in two days' time in a large conference room adjoining a private suite that had been booked in my "pretend" name at the rather luxurious Conrad hotel at Quinta do Lago. Sam and I stayed at my place, and Stephen took over one of my spare bedrooms, with Paul and Richard sharing another, along with the mountains of equipment Richard had brought with him. Stephen said he didn't want anyone to stay at the meeting venue, just in case they were spotted and it got out that there were a lot of important police from various countries congregating at the Conrad. Both Kurt and Markus Dressler, the Chairman of De Beers, who none of us knew previously arrived the following day, and they were both booked under false names into separate suites on different floors at the Tivoli Hotel in Vilamoura. Helena was booked into a suite at Pine Cliffs Resort near Albufeira, while Inspector Paulo Cabrita stayed at his own home. He, like everybody else, would arrive at the Conrad hotel by taxi, dressed in plain clothes with not a uniform in sight.

On Thursday morning—was it a Thursday—to be honest I had no idea as the days just seemed to be flowing into each other. Anyway, as I was saying, on Thursday morning I arrived at the Conrad and collected the key to the conference room we'd booked for our "book publishers" meeting from the girl on reception. Everyone had been told to enter the hotel and turn immediately right into the bar where Sam would be sitting, and she would meet them, give them all a fictitious name badge to show they were representing some fictitious publishing company, and then she gave them directions to the conference room we were using on the top floor. As we'd previously arranged, Paul and Richard, plus all Richard's equipment were the first to arrive and they spent about an hour setting up video equipment, large TV screens, several laptops and various other bits of electronics kit, most of which was totally alien to me, but Richard assured us everything we would need would be at his fingertips as and when we required it. Inspector Paulo Cabrita was the next to knock on the door, and we exchanged friendly handshakes as he entered the room. I did the introductions to Paul and Richard and then Paulo helped himself to an expresso from a large coffee machine we'd had installed in the suite. Helena arrived with Stephen and about three minutes later, Kurt and Markus Dressler arrived. Markus Dressler was a big man in every sense of the word. He was about 6 foot 3 inches tall and was big built. He had a very neatly trimmed beard and moustache, and if I hadn't known better I would have sworn he was a Viking warrior. He also had the booming voice to go with the look. After all the introductions had been completed and coffee had been handed round, we all moved from the suite and into the conference room where we all sat round the large conference table the suite provided.

'Firstly,' began Stephen. 'I would like to thank everyone for coming today, and secondly, if nobody minds—can I please request we all stick to using everyone's Christian names and forget about ranks and titles, it will make life so much easier and quicker in the long run.'

There were general murmurs and nods of agreement and Stephen continued.

'Paulo has kindly asked me to chair the meeting as the Metropolitan police have been involved in this matter since the original murder here in the Algarve, and we probably know more than most about what's been going on to date. My particular thanks to Markus for coming all this way and offering De Beers's full cooperation.'

'Thank you, Stephen,' replied Markus Dressler. 'I must say I was puzzled when Kurt here asked for a confidential meeting with me, but during that meeting he gave me enough information to guarantee my presence here this morning. I was greatly shocked to discover the extent of the involvement of some of my own staff, but please be assured—De Beers will do everything we can to help bring all those involved to justice.'

'Thank you, Markus,' said Stephen. 'We have put together an outline presentation of everything that has happened to date, along with any relevant actions the various people in this room have taken, the information gathered, and the conclusions we've reached as to who the guilty parties are.'

'Everyone,' interjected Paul, 'please feel free to give more information as we go along, but please don't jump ahead. We want everyone to be fully in the picture, and after Stephen and I have finished our initial presentation, we will then hand the meeting over to Michael who suggested we all meet in the first place, and he has suggested a plan of action that will hopefully bring all these bastards to justice.'

'So,' said Stephen taking over again, 'this all started when Malcolm Tisbury, an English diamond dealer and jeweller living here in the Algarve, was found murdered by his cleaner and she called the GNR, which is the police here in the Algarve.'

'As the senior officer for the area, I was appointed to take charge because it was a murder,' said Paulo, 'and when I arrived at the scene I found the message 'Die engleză milionar de porc' written on the wall in Malcolm Tisbury's blood. Translated from the Romanian in which it was written, the message read "Die English Millionaire Pig". As it so happens Malcolm Tisbury's gardener, a Mr Alexandru Dumitrescu is Romanian, and on the floor alongside him we found Mr Dumitrescu's gardening knife—covered in Mr Tisbury's blood. To me it was obviously a set up, but I had to arrest Mr Dumitrescu just in case.'

I felt it was time to add my point of view, so I spoke up.

'I was asked by my gardener, who is also a Romanian and a close friend of Mr Dumitrescu, if I would look into it. He knew I had written a few murder mysteries and assumed I could help. I went to see Sam here who I knew had been a police surgeon back in the UK and she agreed to help me, and together we went to see Inspector Cabrita at the GNR office.'

'Paulo showed us a few photographs,' said Sam, 'taken at the scene…'

'Strictly off the record as you English say,' said Paulo.

'Of course,' I said, and everybody smiled.

'…and I,' continued Sam, 'immediately recognised the revolting knife work on the victim's throat as being that of an English murderer I had come across several years earlier when I was still working with the Metropolitan Police.' Richard put up various photographs of Malcolm's crime scene on the giant TV screen.

'I'm sorry,' interjected Markus, 'who are the Metropolitan Police?'

‘Oh that’s us—the London Police,’ replied Paul.

‘Then why aren’t you called the London Police?’ asked Markus. ‘That way everybody would know straight away who you are?’

‘Please don’t ask, Markus,’ said Paulo, ‘The British are the British, and they have their strange little customs and I’ve always found it is much easier to not ask questions.’ We all laughed and Sam continued.

‘As you can see,’ she said as Richard projected the relevant photograph onto the screen, ‘the knife cuts on Malcolm’s throat are neither the normal slashing type or a straightforward cut, but the killer has taken his time and made a pattern across his throat reminiscent of that made by dressmakers pinking shears. I’d seen this once before, and to me that immediately said our man is a known murderer by the name of Freddie Drayton.’

‘Now Freddie Drayton,’ said Stephen, ‘disappeared about ten years ago and we had no idea where he went. He’d done a bit of freelance work for various gangland bosses, but he’d mostly worked for a gang of jewel thieves led by a man named Derek Simpson, and it seemed to us that this murder and robbery had all the hallmarks of the Simpsons.’

‘I’d been Malcolm Tisbury’s doctor for the last few years,’ said Sam, ‘and I knew through talking to him that he’d been involved in the diamond trade.’

‘That gave us another link to the Simpsons,’ said Paul, ‘but it didn’t help us find them. We knew they’d done a flit to the Costa del Crime…’

‘I’m sorry again,’ said Markus, ‘they’d done a what to the where?’

‘No, I’m sorry, Markus,’ said Paul. ‘Richard, can you put up a map of southern Spain please.’ Addressing Markus again

Paul continued, 'A flit is a word we use to describe a quick movement, in this case a quick getaway, and we call the southern coast of Spain the "Costa del Crime" as that is where ninety percent of British criminals fled to during the sixties and seventies when they were in danger of getting caught by the police. Spain in those days was seen as a safe haven as there was no extradition treaty, and most of them ended up buying flashy villas near Marbella on the bit of Spain called the Costa del Sol, or as we nicknamed it—the Costa del Crime. There is an extradition treaty in place now, but it can take years just to get a case into court, during which time the criminals head off to some other sunny destination that has no extradition agreement with the UK such as Dubai or the Maldives.'

'So,' continued Stephen, 'we were pretty sure it was the work of Freddie Drayton under the guiding hand of Derek Simpson. The problem was finding them and proving they did it.'

'Sam and I headed off to Malcolm's London jewellers shop in Hatton Garden,' I continued, 'and we had a conversation with his shop manager—a Mr Jeremy Green. He told us that there should have been two and a half million pounds worth of uncut diamonds in Malcolm's safe which had been delivered to him by your Pieter Van Straaten, who we gathered was their usual courier from De Beers, and who supplied all of Malcolm's uncut stones.'

Markus slowly nodded indicating he knew of Pieter Van Straaten.

'We concluded,' said Sam, 'that without doubt, the Simpsons must have known about the stones, and that meant they must have had inside information. But we had no idea who that information came from, whether Pieter Van Straaten was involved or just an innocent bystander, but the one thing we did know however was that for all of his criminal life, Derek Simpson had used the same tame lawyer - a man named Dominic St Clair. Would you believe it—we then discovered that Dominic St Clair also happened to be the lawyer for the woman that had inherited ninety percent of Malcolm's business—a certain Caroline Chambers, his God daughter?'

'Now neither of us believe in coincidences,' I said, 'and when Jeremy Green told us that he was getting the other ten percent of the business and also let it slip that Dominic St Clair was flying in to meet with him, alarm bells started ringing in both our heads.'

'Green also mentioned that St Clair was returning to Spain immediately after their meeting,' said Sam, 'so Michael and I decided we had to be at Málaga airport when he landed, follow him and see where he took us. That happened to be a rather nice villa in the town of Mijas which is in the hills just north of Marbella.' As Sam was speaking Richard put a more detailed map of southern Spain on the screen and I pointed out exactly where Mijas was located. Then above the map Richard put up the faces of all five members of the Simpson gang and Dominic St Clair with their names underneath.

'OK, I think I get it so far,' said Markus, 'but obviously my main concern is De Beers and the South African link, and was Pieter Van Straaten crooked and in on it?

'Oh he was as crooked as they come Markus,' I replied, 'but sadly he wasn't the only De Beers employee involved. Sam and I chatted it through and decided the next thing we had to do was to find out where their information was coming from, and after speaking to Stephen, he said that meant getting Interpol involved and the pair of us taking a trip to South Africa.'

Sam took up the story. 'So we flew to South Africa and met up with your Marius Van der Byl, who—for the benefit of those of you that don't know—is De Beers Director for New Business.'

'Please, don't tell me Marius is involved in this—I've known him for over twenty years and would have trusted him with my life.'

'You still can, Markus. Please don't worry—Marius was incredibly helpful and we're sure he knew absolutely nothing about the plots to defraud your clients. No, the man you want and the one who ran the show from South Africa is Francois Viljoen, your Courier Manager. As far as we can tell, Viljoen, along with Pieter Van Straaten and Jan Joubert are the only three De Beers employees involved.'

'But why on earth haven't they been arrested. I know for a fact that all three of them are still working for De Beers, although one of them has now gone part time.'

'The problem is, Markus,' said Kurt, 'Interpol can arrest them anytime, but there is no physical evidence and no proof that they are involved. My face, and that of most of Interpol's investigators are well known by most criminals, and you have to realise that they study us as much as we study them, hence Michael and Sam's excellent under-cover work.'

'So I have to keep on paying these bastards knowing that they are stealing from us?'

'For the moment, Markus—yes please,' replied Stephen. 'But Michael has a plan that will hopefully flush them out and bring the whole lot of them to justice.'

'And that includes the people we haven't even mentioned yet,' said Paul.

'God, how many more people are there involved in this?' asked Paulo.

'Well one of the other things we wanted to know,' I said, 'was what they were doing with all of their ill-gotten gains, and to cut a long story short it meant Sam and I sadly had to spend some time in the Bahamas.'

'My God,' mused Paul, 'the things you two have to sacrifice for your country. I don't know, the Algarve in Portugal, the Costa del Sol in Spain, the Cape in South Africa, and now the Bahamas—it must be incredibly tough being you two.'

'Ignoring the very rude and sarcastic man on my left,' Sam continued as everyone smiled, 'we had discovered through some nifty research carried out by Stephen and his team that Jeremy Green and Caroline Chambers were both directors of a property company named Thaxted Property Holdings in the Bahamas. Michael and I spent a few days there, visited their head office during the day posing as a wealthy couple looking for a property, and then we revisited them again in the early hours of the morning, along with a friend of Kurt's.'

'I should point out at this time,' began Kurt, 'that in order to obtain information not generally available, Interpol occasionally resorts to using highly skilled individuals that haven't always been on the straight and narrow—not that we would ever admit it if asked.'

'Goes without saying old chap,' said Stephen.

'As we were saying,' continued Sam. 'The outfit we broke into in the Bahamas—Thaxted Property Holdings—is an offshore company run on behalf of its owner by a very attractive and astute young lady named Naomi Gardiner. We had spent some time in Amsterdam with Helena earlier, and discovered that the stolen stones all go to Hannes de Jaeger, one of the best, if not the best diamond cutter and polisher in

Holland. The finished stolen stones are mounted in various incredibly expensive pieces, and then sold via the top end Hatton Garden jewellery shop Jeremy Green is involved with in London. The money made from the sale is then invested by Naomi Gardiner and her team in high end property all over the world—villas and estates each worth several million pounds.'

'My God,' sighed Markus, 'it sounds like their operation is beginning to rival ours.'

'Well I don't think it's quite that big yet,' said Stephen, 'but we need to get these bastards before it is. Michael, can you kindly please tell us what you have in mind?'

Chapter Twenty-Six

I opened my notebook and began.

'My idea is basically very simple. We put something in front of them that is so tasty they simply couldn't refuse, and then we catch them in the act. I suggest we make it known through Francois Viljoen that a delivery of thirty million pounds worth of stones is being taken by a single courier to the Algarve for a new customer.'

'Sorry to interrupt your flow, Michael,' said Markus, 'but thirty million is nowhere near enough, and we'd never send a single courier for any amount of stones valued at over ten million sterling. Can I suggest we send a large odd number—say three hundred and seventy five million and we use three couriers?'

'Fine, Markus, you know the numbers far better than me, but won't that make it more difficult for them to steal the stones with three couriers, and therefore less tempting?'

'Yes, it might do, but if we were to use less than three couriers for such an amount it would become highly suspicious.'

'Could we use a couple of our own men as couriers?' asked Stephen.

'Not unless they can pass as South Africans,' replied Markus. 'Do any of your men speak fluent Afrikaans without an accent Stephen, as that is a basic requirement of all our couriers? Plus, our couriers have to spend two years training before we let them loose on international flights with stones for a client.'

'Oh, I see. Well obviously not. Tell me—do you have three couriers you could send who are beyond reproach, and would therefore not help the thieves?'

'I'm sorry to interrupt, Stephen,' I said, 'but I don't think you get the idea. This has to look totally legit to Viljoen, and my understanding is that he, as the courier manager, always selects which couriers to send on which jobs. He has to be left free to do that, but even if all three of them are bent, we will obviously ensure there are enough good guys waiting for them in the Algarve to ensure they don't get away with anything.'

'Would you need to use real uncut stones, Markus,' asked Paul, 'three hundred and seventy five million is a vast amount of money. Couldn't you just say they are the real thing and send paste or whatever you use for fakes?'

'No, they would have to be the real thing,' answered Markus. 'As I said, all our couriers undergo extensive training over two years in which they learn an awful lot about uncut diamonds. They would recognise fakes immediately. What's more, I'm afraid that Francois Viljoen and all the couriers involved in the delivery have to sign detailed documentation which states that they have seen and examined the stones they are taking before they leave, and then the client has to countersign the same documentation to say that they have received them.'

'OK, so back to you, Michael. What's next in this plan of yours?'

'Well I'm hoping Paulo that you can help us with this one. I want to set up a very plush looking high end jewellery shop in the foyer of the hotel here—the Conrad. That's why I chose this place for our meeting. We need to have somewhere that plans to sell the diamonds, and as this is supposed to be a first delivery to new clients, we ought to show off to the world that we have new premises from which to sell our wares, and where better than the most expensive hotel in the Algarve? I assume Markus that you could supply us with some beautiful photography of your wares that we can display on site prior to the grand opening?'

'Oh, that is not a problem. I can send you lots of wonderful photography of beautiful stones in glorious yellow and white gold settings that will make everyone's mouth water. I would also like to offer on behalf of De Beers to finance this entire operation. It is all being done for our benefit, and that is the least we can do. Spend whatever you need to in order to make it look genuine and bring these wretched people down.'

'Thank you, Markus,' said Stephen, 'that is extremely generous of you.'

'I'm sure I can get the Conrad to co-operate, Michael,' said Paulo, 'but what are you going to do about staffing your new shop. You and Sam can't be involved—you're both too well known here in the Algarve, and from what you say Helena and Kurt are both known to at least one or two of the criminals in question as well.'

'Well there shouldn't be any danger to the staff in the Conrad,' I said, 'and I'm sure we can get some beautiful looking models in for a few weeks to parade around the foyer giving out expensive looking leaflets and brochures about the opening night and the wondrous opening night discounts that will be on offer. We don't actually have to do too much other than employ a few models and get in a team of shop fitters to make it look good. I would think the stones won't be delivered to the Conrad anyway, but to somewhere considered very safe, such as a bank.'

'Won't that put the thieves off?' asked Sam

'If we make the package look tempting enough, and with Viljoen's own chosen men involved, I don't think they'll be able to resist going for it. I mean, three hundred and seventy five million pounds. I'm even tempted to have a go for it myself.' I joked.

'They'll probably attempt to steal the stones during the transportation phase anyway,' said Kurt, 'but we can have our own men on the aircraft from South Africa, box in the car using several unmarked cars of our own etc., etc. The important thing is that it must look one hundred percent genuine from beginning to end.'

'OK,' said Stephen. 'So when does this go down?'

'I think we'll need at least two months to get everything and everyone in place,' I said. 'So can I suggest nine weeks today. That'll make it…um Friday the 18th.'

We carried on talking for another couple of hours, making our plans and allocating tasks, and ended up appointing Richard as the main coordinator for "the sting" as we started calling it, since he mostly operated in the backroom in London and nobody would recognise him. There was very little for Sam and me to do in the Algarve, but our main task was to ensure the Simpson's knew of the wonderful opportunity being set up for them. The easiest way of ensuring that they knew all about it was to tell Naomi all the glorious details face to face, and that meant reinstating our previously cancelled trip to Venice. Sam and I left the conference room, walked into the suite, closed the door and with a slightly nervous feeling, I dialled Thaxted's head office in the Bahama's and asked to speak to Naomi Gardiner. She came on the line almost immediately.

'Michael, great to hear from you, and how is poor Sam? She looked absolutely dreadful when I last saw you, and then when I called at your hotel to see you both again, I gathered you'd checked out and left no forwarding address?'

'I'm so sorry Naomi. Sam was feeling absolutely terrible and insisted that she wanted to die in her own bed. Sam's always been a bit of a drama queen, and it's easier to just agree with her than argue.' Sam made a very rude gesture at me and smiled. 'Anyway,' I continued, 'she's fine now, and that's why I'm ringing you. I don't suppose that three story canal-side property in Venice you told us about is still available?'

'Yes Michael—it is. I can fly over anytime to show you round. Where are you at the moment?

'Well at the moment we're staying at the Conrad in the Algarve for a few days, but we can be in Venice on Monday if that's any good?'

'Fantastic!' exclaimed Naomi. 'I'll fly out on Sunday and overnight in Venice. Any chance we could meet up for a meal in Venice on Sunday night and I can give you the history of the property before we go to view it on Monday.

'That sounds great,' I replied enthusiastically. 'I've got your email address and I'll send you our hotel details as soon as I've booked somewhere.'

'That sounds perfect. If you don't know Venice very well Michael, can I recommend you stay at the glorious Gritti Palace? It occupies one of the loveliest spots on the Grand Canal, looking across to the magnificent Salute Church. Its own Club de Doge restaurant has one of the most beautiful dining rooms in Venice looking out over the Grand Canal, with the option at this time of year of eating on the outdoor terrace on the Canal itself. The food is wonderful and definitely a step up from burger and chips at Lucaya Market. The Palace has always been our hotel of choice in Venice and I'm sure you'd love it.'

'That sounds just fantastic,' I replied.

'Look, I'll tell you what,' said Naomi, 'I have to book a room for myself, so why don't I book a double overlooking the Grand Canal for you and Sam at the same time, and if you end up buying our property you can have the cost of the room on us?'

'How can I possibly refuse?' I meekly said, submitting to Naomi's vocal charm attack.

'OK then, I'll look forward to seeing you both in Venice Michael, and please give Sam my love. See you both on Sunday evening. Bye for now.' With that the line went dead. As we walked back into the conference room, I said to Sam: 'I'm sure that woman fancies you.'

'Oh well,' grinned Sam, 'who can blame her?'

I smiled and shook my head as we walked back into the conference room and explained our arrangement with Naomi Gardiner.

'While you've been off spending more of Interpol's money on flashy hotels,' said Stephen, 'we've all been working hard on a couple of ideas.'

'Sorry to correct you, sir,' interrupted Richard, 'but isn't it Mr Dressler's money they're now spending on flashy hotels? Just for the sake of accuracy you understand, sir.'

'Cheeky sod,' glowered Stephen, and then he smiled.

'Richard is however quite right,' said Markus looking directly at Sam and myself.

'It is De Beers's money you are reluctantly now being forced to spend on these dreadful hotels you have been forced to slum it in, and then on top of that you are forced to consume food you would ideally not eat, and partake of wine you would ideally not drink. Am I right or am I right?'

'Oh, you are so right, Markus,' said a very dour Sam, who then burst out laughing.

'Please don't encourage them, Markus, they're bad enough as it is,' said Stephen.

'Anyway,' I interrupted, 'what are these great ideas you've all been working on.'

'Well,' said Paulo, 'we have to justify to Viljoen and his team, and also the Simpsons why De Beers are shipping three hundred and seventy five pounds worth of stones to the Algarve.'

'I have suggested,' said Markus, 'that along with your own new bogus company, we put together a consortium of top end, high class jewellers from around the world who would like to have access to the Algarve market, which let's be honest, in this part of the world is very much a millionaires playground. I can talk to some of our top jewellers that have no outlet in Europe at the moment, and I'm sure I can get enough of them to put their name behind such a venture if De Beers are taking all the risks. That way it is one hundred percent legitimate if the Simpson's try to check it out.'

'I can put the various jeweller's names all over the publicity material and ensure that their staff know to confirm the launch show here at the Conrad,' said Paul.

'But more importantly,' said Stephen, 'none of them must know anything about the sting until it is all over. That way there's no chance of a leak.'

We continued talking and planning for another hour, and then Sam and I went back to my villa and booked the first flight we could to Venice.

Chapter Twenty-Seven

We arrived in Venice just before noon on the Saturday, and checked into the Hilton Garden Hotel which is located just outside Venice, and after lunch we took the short cab ride into Venice itself and jumped onto a "vaporetta" which are the water buses that run up and down the Venetian canals. We managed to find a couple of seats together at the rear of our particular vaporetta and gazed—like most other awe-struck tourists seeing Venice for the first time—at the wonderful sights this unique city has to offer its millions of visitors. We followed the throng and eventually got off at St Mark's Square. On hearing an orchestra playing, we decided to order a couple of small beers, sit and listen to the music for a while and soak up the atmosphere. I love classical music—well actually that's not a hundred percent true. I love a lot of classical music, but the one notable exception for me is operatic singing, which to my ears mostly sounds like cats being drowned. There are rare exceptions of course such as Delibes' wonderful "Flower Duet" for two female voices from his opera "Lakme", the incredibly stirring aria "Nessun Dorma" from "Puccini's" opera "Turandot"—unfortunately best known to most people these days as the music for the football World Cup played in Italy back in 1990, when Bobby

Robson was the England Manager, and Paul Gascoyne cried after being booked, meaning he would miss the next match.

Entrance to the Grand Canal, Venice

The Terrace Restaurant at the Gritti Palace Hotel, Grand Canal, Venice

St Mark's Square and the Doge's Palace (Palazzo Ducale), Grand Canal, Venice

The Rialto Bridge, Grand Canal, Venice

Anyway, back to the present day where we both recognised the music being played as "Spring" from Vivaldi's "Four Seasons". This was hardly surprising as Vivaldi was born in Venice and it is his most famous work. I have to say, the musicians were excellent, and so we took our time over our two small beers, which was just as well as we later discovered when the waiter brought us the bill—they were eleven euros each, but then that's St Mark's Square for you.

We enjoyed the rest of our day getting to know the city, then went back to the Hilton for a meal and a good night's rest. Around ten o'clock on Sunday morning, we got up, had a leisurely breakfast and then got a taxi to the main vaporetta terminal in Venice ready for our journey to the Gritti Palace. For a start, our arrival was to be by boat—not a vaporetta, but by a speedboat to be exact. These wonderful all wooden hulled craft are actually Venice's versions of a taxi; basically the vaporetta are the buses and the speedboats are the taxis. When we arrived at the Gritti Palace, we were met at the boat dock by a wonderfully polite man who spoke perfect English and seemed to know who we were without being told. We then stepped off the water taxi onto the boat dock. Being a wooden boat dock, I expected to be standing on wood, but as I looked down I saw and felt a luxurious thick-pile royal blue carpet under my feet. We were escorted through the entrance and informed by the beautifully dressed staff at the reception desk that Naomi, a regular client at the Palace had given up her usual suite for us, and consequently we had been booked into the opulent Somerset Maugham Royal Suite. Maugham had apparently been a frequent guest at the Gritti Palace, and if money is no object, you can understand why. Our suite of rooms was massive and had five floor-to-ceiling French doors that opened onto a wonderful balcony that ran the full length of the suite, and it afforded truly magical views of the Grand Canal in every direction. I later discovered that the cost of this total luxury experience was over ten-thousand euros a night, and thank God Interpol had provided us with a Gold American Express Card to cover any expenses, which like our passports, was in our false names. One thing I did know for sure—the Gritti Palace was far beyond my meagre wallet's reach. It was a glorious sunny afternoon and so we decided to sit outside on the terrace and share a bottle of wine. We'd talked all this through back at the conference room before we left and Markus was adamant that we had to act like money meant nothing to us, and that we should simply order the best of everything.

'After all,' he'd said, 'that's what I do!'

So having been given the details in advance by Richard, and God knows how he knew all this stuff—but he just seemed to—, we ordered a bottle of "Masseto Toscana IGT", a red Merlot from Tuscany that costs over six hundred euros a bottle. Giovanni, the waiter introduced himself when he came to take our order and didn't even blink when I ordered the wine. He was back two minutes later with our bottle and three glasses.

'Oh Giovanni, you've brought three glasses I see—are you joining us?

'Sadly no, Signore,' he smiled. 'Your friend Miss Naomi has just arrived, and she said she would join you both here on the terrace for a drink as soon as she has been to her room.'

'Excellent,' exclaimed a smiling Sam. 'Thank you Giovanni.'

Giovanni left us alone on the terrace and as he departed, I whispered to Sam.

'Right, I guess the next act in our little play is about to begin.'

'You both made it,' suddenly came a voice from behind us, and Naomi walked out onto the terrace behind us. She looked immaculate in a royal blue two piece skirt and jacket over a white blouse and she was all smiles and bonhomie, or should I say "bonomia" as we were in Italy. We both stood and walked over to greet her, and she gave us both a long hug to be followed by a kiss on each cheek—European style.

'Isn't Venice simply amazing!' she exclaimed with obvious relish. 'I simply adore this city and could quite happily live and work here if only the weather was like this all year.'

'Great to see you again,' I said, 'I assume you'll join us for a glass of wine.'

'Ah, the wonderful Masseto, but one bottle isn't going to go very far between three of us is it?' And with that she turned to face the entrance and called, 'Giovanni, another bottle of the Masseto please. Thank you.'

The one thing you had to say about Naomi—she is always extremely polite.

'We're both really excited about seeing the house tomorrow,' enthused Sam. 'Is it far from here?'

'No, it's literally a couple of canals away. I tell you what, we'll finish our wine and then we can take one of the Palace's water taxis and go and have a look at the outside of it.'

'That would be great,' I said.

'Now tell me,' said Naomi, 'what have you two been up to since I last saw you?'

'It's really exciting!' exclaimed Sam. 'Do you remember, Michael told you I loved really expensive jewellery, you know, diamonds, rubies, emeralds, gold, platinum etc. Ooh, even the names make me shiver with excitement.'

'Yes, I remember you saying,' said Naomi with a very interested look on her face.

'Well anyway, we found out that a consortium of the world's top jewellery companies are going to launch a big brand new outlet at the Conrad Hotel in the Algarve, and we decided to join them and open our own jewellery business there.'

'Of course!' I jumped in before Naomi could say anything, 'we'll have to get in quite a few experts to look after it all and run it for us, but Sam's decided she wants to sell top end pieces using mainly yellow gold and diamonds. We're currently looking for top designers, cutters and all the other people we need, and De Beers in South Africa have agreed to sell us a hundred million pounds worth of uncut stones.'

'Have you heard of De Beers?' queried Sam.

'Yes,' smiled Naomi, 'the name rings a bell, but to be honest it's not really my area of expertise, and I know very little about diamonds—apart from I like wearing them of course.'

'We know very little at this stage ourselves,' I said, 'but it gives Sam something to get her teeth into, and the De Beers people seem incredibly helpful. They even offered to add our order to the consortium's main order for uncut stones. The launch is going to feature a big display of "before and after" with hundreds of millions of pounds worth of uncut stones and hundreds of million pounds worth of top pieces from all the various consortium members.'

'I don't think you should be saying all this, Michael,' said a nervous Sam, 'the man from De Beers said we shouldn't broadcast it to strangers.'

'Well Naomi's hardly a stranger is she dear?'

We all laughed and I quickly changed the subject with us having sewn the seed, and having made sure Naomi had received enough information to pass on to her own consortium—of diamond thieves.

'So Naomi,' I asked, 'where is this canal with our potential new property?'

'Yes,' she said, draining her glass. 'Let's head off.'

Giovanni called the Concierge, who was beautifully adorned from head to toe in a sparkling white uniform, and he in turn spoke into a hand held radio. Fifteen seconds later, one of the Palace's own speed boats pulled up and moored at the boat dock.

The property we went to view was quite an old house, originally built by a Venetian Merchant in the late seventeenth century. I thought it looked incredibly run down and in my opinion if it had been anywhere but here in Venice it wouldn't have been worth more than seven-hundred thousand euros. Obviously I kept my thoughts to myself.

'As you can see,' began Naomi, 'the building is basically in three sections, with two three-storey high sections on either side of the central four stories. It is just off the Grand Canal in the Rio de San Polo. Externally, it is in need of plastering and painting, and there are several companies in Venice that specialise in the restoration work needed, but once completed it will be magnificent. At the moment it only has a few small Juliet style balconies, but you could easily add a full width balcony like those at the Gritti Palace, and you would then get great views of the Grand Canal. Also as you can see, there is a large roof garden on the section nearest the Grand Canal, which already offers great views of the canal. I'll show you round inside tomorrow and you'll see that the inside has been looked after and renovated to a very high standard.'

'If you don't mind me asking, Naomi,' I began, 'if your company owns the building, why didn't you plaster and paint it yourselves?'

'Firstly, we would have had to have spent a fortune, and then if the new owners wanted to repoint all the brickwork and not use plaster, or if they didn't want to plaster every floor, but just the top, or perhaps plaster and paint the central section and repoint the two sides, we'd have to undo all our hard work. What colour should we paint the plaster? White, pink, pale blue, cream who knows what the client will prefer. It's much easier to let the client decide what they want, and the cost of the restoration work is reflected in the property's low price.'

'You didn't tell us the cost of the restoration, Naomi,' queried Sam.

'No I didn't. I'm afraid the cost is the cost, Sam, and it all depends on what you are having done. All our properties are priced at what we consider to be fair, and if a potential client isn't happy with the price, then someone else will be. We've sold over three billion pounds worth of properties in the last ten years Sam, and the price has never been a problem or a sticking point.'

'Well, I love what I've seen so far,' I said, 'and I can't wait to see inside it tomorrow. Somehow I don't think the price is going to be a problem or sticking point for us either.'

The speed boat turned through a hundred and eighty degrees and headed back to the Gritti Palace, where we bade Naomi a temporary farewell until we were due to meet at 8 pm for dinner on the terrace.

Once in our room we got showered and dressed as we chatted over what we'd learnt, and tried to decide if we'd dropped enough information to get Naomi's juices flowing. We decided we had, and neither us nor Naomi mentioned diamonds once throughout the meal. We referred occasionally to good old dad, otherwise known as Sir Colin Philips, and I told her lots of made up stories about how he made his eight billion in various oil fields all over the world until he sold the lot to a mysterious Russian oligarch who we'd never met. To be honest, we had a very pleasant evening and bade her goodnight around eleven- thirty.

The following morning we went to view the property, and I have to say true to her word, it was absolutely magnificent inside. We made lots of 'Ooh' and 'Aah' noises as we went from room to room, and at the end of the tour, we confirmed that we wished to purchase our very own chunk of Venetian real estate. I gave Naomi the address Kurt had set up for us where all the paperwork should be sent as he was dying to read an official Thaxted property contract. He felt sure it would undoubtedly contain bank information and other goodies he could get his teeth into. We went back to the Gritti Palace, where we shared another bottle of the excellent Masseto, now that we were clients. Like everything else on this trip, the bill was paid by Thaxted. I confirmed that we would fly out to the Bahamas with our lawyers once all the paperwork was ready to sign, having arranged in advance an international bank transfer for eighteen million pounds.

Chapter Twenty-Eight

We flew back to the Algarve and met up with Stephen, Paul, Richard, Helena and Kurt who were all now staying in the Algarve until the "sting" was over. They had taken two suites, one of which had a conference room attached, at the Tivoli Hotel in Vilamoura that overlooked the Marina. They were all booked in as a group of air conditioning salesmen and they kept mostly to the rooms. They felt it was far safer to stay put in the Algarve and not run the risk of constantly flying in and out of Faro airport, where they might be recognised by anyone on the lookout for the comings and goings of anyone connected to the law. Paulo had told us at our previous meeting that there was usually a member of some gang or other on constant lookout at the airport, and they would then spread the word around the criminal fraternity if any foreign police or Interpol officers were spotted. As Stephen had previously told us in Greenwich, the crooks study the police just as much as the police study the crooks.

Over the next two or three weeks, Sam and I did very little other than swim and catch up with sleep back at the villa, and once we'd rested up, we were raring to go again. On the Tuesday morning of that week, the phone in the villa rang, and it was Stephen requesting our presence at the hotel. Apparently there had "been a development". We drove down to the Tivoli and headed up to the top floor which was where their rooms were. We knocked on the door and saw the peephole go dark as someone on the other side put their eye to it. Paul opened the door and we went in. Paulo had already joined everyone and we all went through to the conference room and sat down round the conference table.

'We've got wind of something this morning which we are pretty sure involves our friends in Mijas,' began Stephen, 'but I'll hand over to Kurt as it was his team that came up with the information.'

'After our last meeting I asked Interpol if we could have the necessary funding could be made available to put tails on some of the people involved, and to my surprise, they readily agreed. So we immediately put a tail on the Simpsons.'

'If they split up at any point,' interrupted Stephen, 'then we've decided to concentrate on Sandra as we now think she runs the whole shebang.'

'I'm sorry, Stephen,' asked Paulo, 'but what is shebang? This is not a word I know.'

'Sorry Paulo, it's an American phrase dating back to the 1920's. It's similar to another American phrase "the whole kit and caboodle" which like "shebang" means everything, the lot etc. In other words, we now think Sandra Simpson runs everything.'

'And you English tell me Portuguese is hard to learn.'

We all laughed as Kurt took over the conversation again.

'As well as the Simpsons, we've put tails on Dominic St Clair, Francois Viljoen in Cape Town, Jeremy Green in London and a guy named Jamal Bashara who we believe is an arms dealer operating out of Dubai. All I can say is thank God we did.'

'Why, what's happened?' asked Sam

'On Saturday, our tail followed Dominic St Clair to Málaga airport where St Clair caught a flight to London Gatwick. Our tail telephoned it through to me along with the flight details, and I called one of our London team and asked him to tail St Clair once he got off the Gatwick flight and let me know where he went.'

'And where did he go?' I asked

'Initially, he caught a bus that connects London Gatwick airport to Heathrow, London's other main airport. My man caught the same bus and sat at the back reading a newspaper, while watching everything St Clair did. On arriving at Heathrow, St Clair got off and checked in for the Emirates afternoon flight to Dubai.'

'The natural assumption I guess was that St Clair was meeting this Jamal Bashara guy in Dubai?' asked Paul.

'Correct and that's exactly what he did. Our other guy in Dubai followed Jamal Bashara to the airport where they sat in the corner of a coffee shop for three hours. Then St Clair caught the next flight back to London, and Bashara went back to his shop.'

'I assume Bashara's shop doesn't say "Arms Dealer" above the entrance?' asked Sam.

'No it doesn't,' smiled Kurt. 'Jamal Bashara is, and has been a much respected dealer in the world of expensive rolls of silk materials for several years. He has a small to medium sized shop located in the basement of the main shopping mall in Dubai, and we suspect he does his arms business from the office behind the shop.'

'What sort of arms are we talking about Kurt?' I asked.

'Oh he supplies a few machine guns and grenades, but the main armaments he trades in are SAM's, or Surface to Air Missiles. I don't mean the big stuff, but smaller missiles like

Patriots and S-300's, but his two biggest sellers are the short-range portable systems that a man can fire from his shoulder like a rifle, the two most popular being the American Stinger and the Strela-3.'

'I've heard of the Stinger,' said Sam, 'but what's a Strela-3?'

'It's the Russian equivalent,' answered Richard. 'NATO call it the Gremlin. It's quite old technology now as it dates back to the mid 1970's, but it still works well, and that's all that matters to the people that buy this stuff.'

'And who is that, do we know who his clients are?' asked Paul.

'To be frank, Paul, the list is fairly endless. He's not in the least bit fussy. He has over the years sold arms and SAM missiles to Al-Qaeda, ISIS, the Taliban, the Tamil Tigers, Hamas, Hezbollah, Boko Haram and Al-Shabaab. It's a case of "you name them" and I can virtually guarantee they are on his client list.'

'So what's the link between Jamal Bashara and the Simpsons? How do we know they're tied in together?'

'Well St Clair flying all the way to Dubai for a three-hour meeting in a coffee shop and then flying straight back again is a pretty good clue, but we first became aware of Bashara about two years ago. We were asked by your MI6 people if we knew anything about a South African terrorist named Eugene Coetzee, who they suspected of being involved in a bombing incident in Birmingham. Interpol had Coetzee's name on our books after a bombing in Durban, but we couldn't prove anything. Other than our suspicions, the only thing we knew about him was that he flew in and out of Dubai every few months and every time he met with Jamal Bashara.

'So what made you suspicious?' asked Sam.

'As far as we knew,' continued Kurt, 'Bashara was a perfectly legitimate silk merchant, but once we started checking, we realised Coetzee wasn't the sort of guy to be buying rolls of silk. That made us think Bashara was selling something Coetzee needed, and our initial thought was that it was either going to be forged documents or arms. We asked the authorities in Dubai if they had anything on Bashara and they said they'd look into it and come back to us. The UAE is a strange place; their law enforcement agencies are fairly cooperative with Interpol, even though the place is a haven for criminals as none of the United Arab Emirates accept extradition orders. We heard nothing for weeks, and then totally out of the blue, Dubai telephoned us and said they had no definite proof, but they'd been watching Bashara ever since our request, and they were now pretty sure Bashara was somehow involved in the arms trade.

'But that still doesn't explain why you thought the Simpsons were involved,' said Paul.

'Well, we didn't at that stage. It wasn't until the murder of Malcolm Tisbury and the involvement of Michael and Sam here along with yourselves that one of our people started trawling back through all the old files. They came across the name Dominic St Clair and him having visited Bashara on numerous occasions. We put two and two together, started watching everyone involved, and here we are.'

'Wow!' exclaimed Sam, 'so they're diamond thieves, murderers, international money launderers and now arms dealers. What's next I wonder?'

'Well I say we put them all behind bars before they do anything else,' said Stephen.

'If you head down to the Conrad, you'll see the shop fitters are in, and they've started building a massive display area with cabinets in polished steel, rosewood and walnut, and all with triple glazed bullet proof glass. There will be God knows how many armed security guards once the uncut stones and the finished jewellery arrives, but hopefully it won't get that far and the Simpsons will make their move during the transport phase.'

'How do we know they'll try and go for it, or for that matter have even heard about it?' asked Helena.

'Oh I don't think there's much doubt they'll have heard about it,' said Stephen. 'You and Michael laid it on a plate for Naomi Gardiner in Venice, and I'm positive she will have passed it on. We know Francois Viljoen is in the picture because Markus telephoned me to say that Marius Van der Byl, their new business manager, briefed Viljoen last week, and Viljoen has already put the job out to four of his couriers, including Jan Joubert who we know is as bent as a nine bob note.'

'I'm sorry Stephen—a nine bob note?' queried Paulo.

'Sorry Paulo. Old British currency used to include something called a shilling, which was nick-named a bob, and before you ask—I have no idea why. Anyway, the only legal note that the Royal Mint produced was a ten shilling note, or in slang parlance—a ten bob note. So if someone produced a nine bob note it had to be a forgery, or as we say—bent.'

'I think I must en-roll in a language school that teaches me all these things Stephen. Then in twenty years' time I might understand what on earth you are all talking about.'

Everyone laughed, but we all sympathised with Paulo. It was interesting, Stephen wasn't a cockney, and he wasn't even a Londoner as he came from the Home Counties, but he frequently lapsed into the slang used by the criminal fraternity which Stephen informed us was a habit he'd picked up over the years in pubs down the Old Kent Road.

'In addition to all that,' continued Stephen, 'Markus is placing full page glossy colour adverts in both the Portugal News and the Algarve Resident newspapers, the two local weekly newspapers and between the two of them, it will guarantee everyone in the Algarve will know about it. Plus, he is also putting full page colour adverts in the Euro Weekly, Sur and the Costa Del Sol News. Between those three newspapers, that should guarantee all of Andalucía knows about the display, including Mijas.'

'Well, apart from ensuring everything is ready on time at the Conrad,' I said, 'I don't think there's much more any of us can do at this stage.'

How wrong was I?

Chapter Twenty-Nine

The following day I got a telephone call from Stephen asking if Sam and I would go to the Tivoli as he'd got a new travel job for us, but only if we were a hundred percent happy. Our interest was immediately piqued, but he wouldn't say anything else over the phone.

'I bet he wants us to go to Dubai,' I said as we drove to Vilamoura.

'God I'm not sure about that,' exclaimed Sam. 'I don't know, but I would think arms dealers are bloody dangerous types! Surely that's a job for Interpol, not us?'

'Well I may be wrong, but I can't think of what else it could be, and why would he say we had to be a hundred percent happy if it wasn't dangerous. No, it has to be Dubai.' But I was wrong—just for a change!

Paul opened the door and welcomed us in.

'Come in you two and grab a seat. Tea, coffee?'

'Yes please Paul, tea and biscuits for both of us.' I said looking at Sam who nodded.

'I don't want to go to Dubai,' exclaimed Sam. 'Well I do, because I really like it there, but I don't want to get involved with spying on arms dealers—it's too scary. So there. I've said it, and you can't make me change my mind.'

'Good grief,' said Stephen entering the room 'She does go on a bit your other half, doesn't she? Sam dear, there's absolutely no way in the world we'd ask you to go after arm's dealers, that's a job for MI6 and their professionals.'

'Thank God for that!' exclaimed a much relieved Sam. 'I was getting really worried.'

'I'm glad you told me, Sam, or I'd never have noticed,' said a sarcastic Paul smiling.

'No, we want you two to go back to the Bahamas,' continued Stephen. 'Ask to view another property somewhere and make sure Naomi knows all the details about the jewellery and stones being exhibited in the Algarve. Get really excited about it, tell her about all the hundreds of millions of pounds worth of diamonds that will be on display. We've, or should I say your top London based legal team, have in the meantime sent her a load of tricky questions about the property in Venice. That should give us more time before they ask for the money, but in the meantime we thought it would be good if you popped over with the view of buying something else and fed her some more information in order to get her excited and even more determined to get the Simpson's involved in trying to nick the stones.'

'The Bahamas and the lovely Naomi we can deal with,' I said. 'Just don't ask us to get involved with arms dealers. We definitely didn't sign up for that.'

'Look Stephen,' said Sam, 'thinking about what you've just suggested, according to the story we've spun Naomi we already own properties in the UK, Monaco, La Jolla, Klosters, Cape Town and Dubai, and we're now in the process of buying another one in Venice. It seems to me buying even more property would look a bit suspicious, but I did notice when we were there last, that they had a few top of the range yachts on their books. Our pretend selves haven't got one of those, plus the fact that they cost even more money than houses. Why don't we try and buy a yacht from Naomi?'

'Sam, you're a genius,' said Stephen.

'I wouldn't go that far,' I said. I shouldn't have said it, but it just sort of popped out.

'Can I borrow your shoe please, Stephen?' asked Sam.

'Please don't, Stephen,' I begged. 'She wants to throw it at me.'

'I really don't blame her,' said Paul laughing. 'You really are an awful cad, Mr Turner. Do you want to borrow one of my shoes, Sam?' he asked.

'Perhaps later,' said Sam, who gave me a withering look and then thankfully smiled.

'OK, can we please get back to discussing yachts,' requested Stephen, which is exactly what we did for the next hour or so, after which I telephoned Naomi and said we'd like to pop over and see her. She was obviously at first concerned that we wanted to pull out of the Venice deal, particularly after all the difficult questions our lawyers had asked about planning permission etc., but I assured her we were both still very keen on the Venice property and simply wished to consult her about a different sort of purchase we thought she could help us with. She asked what I meant and I explained we liked the idea of buying a yacht, and we'd need a Captain and a crew to go with it, but we needed some guidance as we knew nothing about yachts. As she'd been so helpful with the Venice property and we'd seen various brochures and bits of information on yachts in her office as well, we thought she was the ideal person to ask. We made an appointment to meet in her office the following week.

Five days later, we flew back to the Bahamas, and checked in again at the Grand Lucayan Resort. We'd brought with us some of the amazing publicity material Markus had produced for us including photographs of what the "before and after" exhibit was going to look like.

Markus had put underneath the pile of uncut stones that even as they were, varying shades of brown, shapeless and boring stones—they were nevertheless worth three-hundred and seventy-five million pounds sterling, or over four-hundred million Euros. I have to say, to me they just looked like any pile of stones you could have picked up on Brighton beach, but what did I know. Pictured to the right of them was another pile, and I do mean a pile of beautiful yellow gold and diamond encrusted jewellery. Tiaras, necklaces, rings, pendants, bracelets, broaches, earrings—you name it—it was there, and underneath that incredible pile was printed their value, an amazing six point eight billion pounds. We were pretty sure that if that didn't whet the appetite of the Simpsons, then nothing would.

As we sat in our hotel room staring at the glossy brochures Sam said, 'You know Michael, there's only one problem with showing this brochure to the world.'

'And what's that pray tell,' I replied.

'Something as valuable as this little lot might well attract the interest of numerous other diamond thieves who fancy their chances.'

'True,' I said, 'but don't forget, that fantastic pile of real jewellery won't actually be going on display. It won't even be in the Algarve as it doesn't exist. It's simply a collection of great colour photographs. It's just shown on the publicity in order to whet the Simpson's appetite.'

'Mmm, I'd forgotten that,' said a thoughtful Sam, 'still, the pile of uncut stones will be real enough, and they might well attract other thieves we are totally unaware of.'

'Again, that's true. But don't forget Kurt will have six SSA undercover operatives on the aircraft, and in the Algarve keeping an eagle eye on everything.'

'SSA?' asked Sam.

'Sorry, that's the State Security Agency, South Africa's version of our MI6. As both Kurt and Helena have told us on numerous occasions, all Interpol's men and women are known by most thieves, so he has "borrowed" six of the SSA's top undercover operatives, and they will all be armed with automatic hand guns under their jackets. Kurt said the SSA originally said no to Interpol's request, but then Markus put pressure on them and they caved in. Being chairman of the country's richest company gives him a lot of clout.'

'Just so that I'm a hundred percent sure,' queried Sam, 'what are we actually asking of Naomi, and what's our real objective?'

'Well, we explain that we were chatting a few days ago, and I mentioned watching the Grand Prix in Monaco this year, which we can see from our balcony which overlooks Monte Carlo's marina, and then you said it would be so much nicer if we could watch it from our own yacht moored in the marina. You then started jumping up and down and got really excited saying we ought to buy a brand new yacht. I suggested buying a second hand one, but you said, "For God's sake, Michael, we're billionaires, we don't buy other people's cast offs. No, we must order a new one." Then you remembered seeing lots of yacht magazines and brochures on the big coffee table in Naomi's office, so we thought we'd come and see Naomi and would look at the possibility of ordering a new yacht.'

‘Definitely ordering a new one—not buying an existing one.’

‘No. Stephen said if we just wanted to buy an existing yacht then Naomi could take us to any one of the incredible marinas spread around the Caribbean, all of which are full of multi million pound yachts. It would make it very difficult for us to say we couldn’t find what we wanted. However, if we’re ordering a new yacht, or as the yachting fraternity call it “commissioning” a new yacht, then we can spend forever designing what we want. And you my girl, need to be at your fussiest best, demanding gold plated taps everywhere, fibre optic lighting in all the bathrooms or whatever.’

‘Ooh, that sounds lots of fun,’ laughed Sam, and with that we left the hotel, jumped in the hired Mercedes, and took a leisurely drive to Thaxted’s Bahamas building for our appointment with Naomi.

Chapter Thirty

We were of course expected and Cassandra showed us straight up to Naomi's office. We sat in two of the luxurious armchairs after Naomi had done her usual kissing us on the cheek ritual. Being British and being used to shaking hands with people as the standard greeting, it took me a while to get used to the fact that everybody in Portugal, and most other European countries kiss you on both cheeks. Left then right. Unless of course you are Dutch, in which case it was three kisses—left, right and then left again. Having lived in the Algarve for several years, I was now used to it.

'It's great to see you guys again,' gushed Naomi, 'how is everything?'

'Oh we're having such a great time,' said Sam, gushing just as much as Naomi, 'you know, Naomi, it's such fun designing what we're going to do with the Venice property, but I just can't decide what colour to paint the outside.'

'We've decided we're definitely going to plaster and paint the external walls,' I said, 'it's just agreeing on the colour. I want a rather relaxing cream with white trim, which I feel will blend in with the other buildings, but Sam's very keen on pink.'

'I don't want to blend in, Michael—I want to make a statement.'

'You can get some very subdued pinks that will still make a statement Sam. For example, look at the walls of the Palazzo Pisani Moretta.' As she was talking, she put a Google Earth picture of the Palazzo up on the fifty-five inch TV monitor. It truly was a beautiful building, and I suppose you could call the walls a shade of pink, although to my mind it was more of an apricot colour. Naomi was still talking. 'The façade of the Palazzo Pisani Moretta is, in my mind, one of the most beautiful in Venice. It is a fantastic example of what's known as Venetian Gothic Floral style with its two floors of six-light mullioned windows, all with ogival arches similar to those found in the loggia of the Doge's Palace. As you can see, the central pointed arched doorways open directly on to the Grand Canal. What do you think? Is that pink enough for you Sam?'

'Oh, it's really beautiful, Naomi. It's absolutely gorgeous. We've got to do that Michael—we must have those gothicky flowered window things on our house.'

'If you want them, Sam, you're going to have to be precise when you place the order with the renovation team. As I said, it's called "Venetian Gothic Floral". Would you like me to include the description, along with a photograph of the front façade of the Palazzo Pisani Moretta in my next communication with your lawyers? By the way, they have asked us a multitude of questions, and insist on having written guarantees about planning permission being granted before signing the contracts. It won't be a problem, but it all takes time.'

'Well I'm afraid we're stuck with the lawyers,' I replied. 'It was a strict condition of the inheritance that we could not change the lawyers, and any legal documents or purchases over one million pounds have be scrutinised by the lawyers prior to signature. My father said Sam and I were both what he called "spendthrifts" and it was his way of insuring we weren't broke by the time we were fifty.'

'Enough of all that legal stuff!' exclaimed Sam. 'Can you organise a yacht for us Naomi? I can already see it in my mind's eye. It has to have a long pure white hull with two beautiful royal blue coach lines down the sides, at least ten luxury cabins—including a massive one for us overlooking the front of the boat.'

'You mean the bow of the yacht dear,' I corrected.

'Well I may not know all the technical terms, clever clogs! But I know what I want, and that includes a large lounge, a separate dining room, a massive luxury home cinema, a Jacuzzi on the top deck and a bar.'

'No helipad, Sam?' queried Naomi.

'Ooh,' yelped Sam bouncing up and down in her armchair. 'Of course, I never thought of that. But if we're going to have a helipad we'll need a helicopter to go with it. Can you organise that as well, Naomi?' asked Sam.

'Of course, but it might take a bit of time to find a yacht that meets all those specifications, Sam. Would you both be prepared to do some alterations?' asked Naomi. Sam responded exactly as planned with our well-rehearsed line.

'Good God, Naomi—we're billionaires, we don't buy other people's cast offs. No, we must order a new yacht.'

'Is that something you can help us with?' I asked. 'I'm sorry, Naomi, but I forgot to mention we wanted to order a brand new yacht when we made the appointment. My mind has been so full of Sam's new jewellery enterprise that it just went out of my brain.'

'Yes, I really am so excited,' said Sam. 'You must have a look at our lovely brochure, Naomi. Michael,' instructed Sam, ‘can you please give Naomi one of the brochures De Beers have put together for us.’

‘De Beers eh,’ queried Naomi. ‘Only the best for you and Michael.’

I passed one of the brochures over to Naomi and Sam immediately, and as pre-arranged, jumped in and directed Naomi to page six of the brochure which had the “before and after” exhibition description and photographs.

‘De Beers have been so helpful. They put this great consortium of jewellery companies together, of which our new company will be one, and then can you believe it—they’re sending over all those uncut stones from South Africa. I mean, it’s incredible, but that pile of boring looking rocks is worth three hundred and seventy five million pounds?’

‘I’m sorry, Sam, as I said to you before, I know very little about jewellery, but I would love to look through your brochure later. Any chance I could keep this copy?’

‘Of course,’ I replied. ‘We have several copies with us.’

Great I thought, she’s taken the bait hook, line and sinker, and you can guarantee the second we’ve left, the contents of that brochure will be scanned and emailed to Mijas.

For the next hour and a half, Sam was in her element specifying all the details of her new yacht. My only thought was thank God we can’t afford one for real, as there was just the chance that Sam might actually be like that if money was no object. Ooh. Scary!

We left Naomi’s office and headed back to the Lucaya, where we telephoned Stephen and brought him up to date. We then decided that having achieved our objective of getting Naomi to well and truly take the bait, we’d take a couple of days for ourselves just lying in the sun on the beach, drinking beer and racing over the waves on two of the hotel’s bright yellow and white jet skis. Three days later we arrived back in the Algarve.

Chapter Thirty-One

After a good sleep, we headed down to the Conrad to discover an amazing change had taken place. The foyer now hosted a beautiful series of display cabinets all arranged in a giant interlocking hexagon shape, with a series of lights and invisible laser beams pointing down from what I can only describe as a sparkling crown positioned above the display cases.

At this stage, there was nothing in the display cases, and once we'd finished looking round the foyer we headed upstairs to meet with Stephen, Kurt and co.

'So how was your trip?' began Paul. 'Looking at your suntans I assume you had a two-minute meeting with Naomi and then spent the rest of the time sun bathing on the beach?'

'Close enough,' smiled Sam. 'The meeting with Naomi took nearly four hours, and she asked if she could keep the brochure, so without doubt—she definitely took the bait.'

'So have the Simpsons,' smiled Stephen as Helena brought us two cups of coffee.

'If your meeting with Naomi took four hours and allowing for the time change between the Bahamas and Spain which is an hour ahead of here…' You could almost hear the clogs turning over and going through the gears in Stephen's brain. 'Mmm…' he murmured.

‘What our glorious leader is trying to say,’ interrupted Paul, ‘is that about an hour after your meeting with Naomi finished, Dominic St Clair’s tail followed him all the way here to the Conrad. He came into the foyer, looked at all the work going on, picked up one the brochures, sat and read through it over a G and T in the bar, then he returned to his car and drove back to Mijas. He went straight to the Simpson’s villa clutching the brochure in his hand.’

‘Quite right, Paul,’ said Stephen. ‘That’s exactly what I was going to say.’

‘I’d say they’re going to go for it,’ said Paul.

‘Probably,’ said Stephen, ‘but we can’t know for sure, and if they do decide to go for it, when and where will they hit?’

‘Markus telephoned us yesterday,’ said Paul, ‘to say that Francois Viljoen has notified him of his four chosen couriers; two to carry the stones and two riding shotgun. The four includes Jan Joubert who we know is as crooked as they come, and surprise of surprises, Viljoen said as there is such a large quantity of stones and such a high value involved he intends to accompany the couriers himself.’

‘They would usually fly on South African Airways into London,’ said Stephen, ‘and then take a British Airways flight to Faro. De Beers, like a lot of companies that transport incredibly valuable goods around the world, have arrangements with both airlines that allow them to carry small fire arms in the aircraft’s cabin.’

‘I didn’t think anyone was allowed to carry guns on planes?’ asked Sam.

‘Most people know that in the USA, Federal Air Marshall’s always carry guns on flights, and since 9/11, not all but most international flights in and out of the USA have at least one armed FAM on board. Other countries have their own rules, but unlike the USA, most other countries don't broadcast the fact, and will always deny it if you ask.'

'But De Beers couriers are licensed to carry guns?' continued Sam.

'Again, if you ask, it will be denied, but between you me and the gatepost, guns are carried on flights by a whole host of people; Air Marshalls, FBI agents, Interpol officers, Secret Service agents, certain Police officers, various high risk courier services etc., etc.'

'You said they would usually fly on South African Airways Stephen. Does that mean that this time they're not?'

'Markus is more than happy to help, but he wants to minimalize the risk of success for the Simpsons as much as possible. So the stones and the couriers will all be flying from Cape Town direct into Faro on one of De Beers's private jets.'

'From there,' continued Paul, 'they'll be taken in two unmarked cars to the Millennium bank in Almancil, where they will be kept in the vault overnight. The stones will then be driven in the same two unmarked cars to the Conrad the following morning, and put on display. We're basically offering the two journeys in the unmarked cars as the ideal opportunity to hijack the stones. It will be made known that the main display of finished jewellery accompanied by several armed guards will arrive the next day. That way we hopefully keep the window of opportunity for the theft of the uncut diamonds as small as possible, as we're assuming the Simpsons won't want to take on armed guards. In theory, the exhibition will then officially be open to the public the next day, although it will of course be cancelled whatever happens, as it was never intended to be real anyway, just a ploy to flush out the Simpsons.'

'How do we make sure the Simpsons know about the unmarked cars etc.?' Sam asked.

'Ah, well that's where you two come in again,' replied Stephen. 'We thought you could both head up to Covent Garden, tell Jeremy Green all about your wonderful new jewellery business, and then ask him to become your new sales manager with an absolutely ridiculous salary on offer. At the same time ensure you tell him all about the exciting future the company has, and start with the exhibition details, show him the brochure and make sure you drop in the bit about the stones and the unmarked cars etc.'

'Brilliant idea, Stephen!' exclaimed Sam.

'Well I can't take any of the credit,' said Stephen, 'it was all Helena's idea.'

'As I said—brilliant idea, Helena. So when are we off to London?' I asked.

'No time like the present,' said Paul. 'Well tomorrow actually. We've booked you both on to the early flight tomorrow morning. That gives you plenty of time to go home, pack, eat sleep etc. and be at the airport for the 8:15 flight.'

And that's just what we did. We landed in London just after 11:00 am and arrived at Jeremy Green's Hatton Garden shop by taxi on the stroke of 12:30. Fortunately he was in, along with his two female assistants. The first thing we noticed was that his security had been beefed up, and now included iron grills over the inside of the windows. There had always been signs on the outside stating that the windows were triple glazed bullet proof glass—enough to deter most burglars.

'Well, well,' he greeted us like long lost friends, 'Michael and Sam, how the devil are you both, and are you married yet?'

'We're excellent Jeremy thank you,' replied Sam, 'and no, regarding the second part of your question, he hasn't even asked me yet!' said Sam, giving me a withering look.

'I can't,' I replied. 'I'm scared,' and then in my very best conspiratorial voice, I leaned towards Jeremy and whispered loud enough for Sam to hear. 'She might say yes.'

'If you don't ask me soon, I might just say no,' smiled Sam. 'Anyway Jeremy, we come bearing tidings of great joy.'

'It's not Christmas, Sam,' I said, but she just ignored me and kept talking.

'We told you that we were hoping to open a new jewellery business, possibly in London and possibly in the Algarve.'

'Yes, I remember you telling me,' said Jeremy.

'Well we're doing both. We will be launching the company in the Algarve, and then following that up with a new shop here in Hatton Garden.' Sam dug into her briefcase and pulled out one of the A4 size full colour exhibition brochures. 'We are launching the new company with a fabulous three-day exhibition at the Conrad hotel in the Algarve, and De Beers have done us proud by putting together a big consortium of top jewellery companies from around the world to join us.'

'The consortium,' I said, 'comprises of companies from Brazil, the USA, Canada, South Africa, India, Malaysia, Abu Dhabi, Singapore, New Zealand, Australia and ourselves. They're all companies that buy their diamonds exclusively from De Beers, but currently only sell within their own countries. De Beers's idea is that the exhibition will hopefully help them break into the European market, along with providing a wonderful launch pad for ourselves, and that would obviously mean increased orders for De Beers.'

‘I have to say,’ said Sam, ‘De Beers have been incredibly helpful in putting on this exhibition for us, and you should see the amazing jewellery they are loaning the exhibition. You’ll find all the details on page six of the brochure.’

Jeremy immediately turned to page six in the brochure, and his eyes nearly fell out when he saw the amazing photograph of the pile of jewellery Markus had photographed.

‘It amazes me,’ I said, ‘that that pile of boring looking lumps of rock on page six could end up being turned into all that amazing jewellery shown on page seven.’

Markus had used a well-known publishing trick to give the photograph of the finished jewellery more “pizazz” as he called it, and that was to use “spot lamination” on the parts of the photograph showing the actual jewellery. The rest of the photograph, background, velvet base etc. had no spot lamination and was quite dull in comparison, but this just made the jewellery sparkle even more.

It was at this point we’d agreed in advance that Sam would take over and casually drop the transport details into the conversation.

‘I’m afraid I’m a real fusspot Jeremy, I worry about everything. I mean to say, all those uncut diamonds for example. OK, they are being flown from South Africa to Faro in one of De Beers private jets, but instead of loading them into a well-protected armoured security truck, they’re doing what to me seems very dangerous—they’re simply using two unmarked cars to take them to the bank vault in Almancil overnight, and then from the bank to the Conrad in the morning.’

‘De Beers explained all that darling,’ I said. ‘They felt armoured security trucks would draw too much attention. Anyway, you don’t want to hear about all that surely Jeremy?’

'No, but I can see Sam's point' said Jeremy. 'I mean, are they carrying the stones into the airport for example, where surely anyone could try and steal them?'

'Oh no,' said Sam. 'They are driving the two cars out to meet the aircraft on the tarmac, and then driving the stones straight to the bank in Almancil.'

'Oh I see,' said a very thoughtful Jeremy.

Not wishing to raise any suspicion about the conversation, I felt it was time to change the subject.

'Jeremy,' I said. 'The real reason we've called in to see you was to make you an offer and ask you if you would you would be interested in becoming our European Sales Manager. You know the business, and we don't. You will I'm sure have lots of contacts, but we don't. You have lots of experience, which we don't, and you know how to run a retail jewellers, which we don't. Whatever you are getting paid at the moment, we'll double it if you could start next month, even earlier if possible?'

'I know, why don't you pop over to the Algarve and come to the exhibition,' asked Sam. Another pre-planned part of the conversation. 'Please say yes to our offer, Jeremy,' she squealed.

'Double, wow, that truly is an amazing offer, and I'll definitely give it a lot of thought. As you know, I now own ten percent of this business, but that shouldn't be affected in any way by my not actually working here. Would it be possible to give me a couple of days to think about it, weigh up my options, and then get back to you?'

'Of course,' smiled Sam. 'We really do hope it's a yes, and don't forget, we'd love to see you in the Algarve at our wonderful exhibition.'

Where we can cheerfully arrest you, you creepy little shit, along with all the other murderous bastards in your gang. Well that's what I was thinking, but needless to say, I refrained from saying it out loud. We left the shop, caught a taxi to Victoria station where we hopped on the Gatwick Express. At Gatwick, we caught the next flight out to Faro and arrived at the hotel in the late evening to report that the uncut stones delivery details had been well and truly noted by Jeremy Green.

Chapter Thirty-Two

To be honest, the next two and a half weeks were really boring. Well at least for Sam and me. We had nothing to do except lay in the sun, swim, eat and drink, and we did all of that with great enthusiasm. This week looked as if it was going to be much the same. Meanwhile, the shop fitters were completing their work at the Conrad, and then a team of "finishers" came in. To be honest I didn't know such people existed, but after the shop fitters had left, these people came in, cleared all the rubbish, then cleaned and polished every surface to an unbelievable shine, far better than standard cleaners would have done. Then on Wednesday morning, I received a call on my mobile from Kurt.

'Good morning Michael, can you and Sam get over here to the hotel and come and join us as soon as possible. We have news.'

We got changed out of our pool clothes into something more suitable and raced over to the hotel in my car. We jumped in the lift and headed up to the conference room. As we arrived, Helena was serving coffee to everyone, and then we sat at the table with everybody else.

'Thank you for racing over here you two, and my apologies to everybody else for making you wait, but I didn't want to have to repeat myself and keep on going over this.'

'No problem, Kurt,' said Stephen, 'but now we are all here, can you please spit it out.'

'As you know,' began Kurt, 'we've had tails on various people for a few weeks now, and in addition we've been listening in to Francois Viljoen's phone calls and getting copies of his texts. Until this morning there had been nothing to report, but just over an hour ago, Viljoen telephoned Dominic St Clair. Richard, can you play the recording please?'

'Of course,' and Richard pressed play.

'Dominic St Clair,' said the lawyer in his best legal voice.

'Good morning Dom.'

'Oh, hi Francois.'

'Listen. I've got the information we needed. There will be two unmarked cars driven out to meet the plane on the tarmac. There will be a driver and someone riding shotgun in each car. They'll be two E class Mercedes, one black and one silver. I'm informed Mercs are two a penny in the Algarve, so they won't stand out.'

'I'll let everyone know.'

'There will be four couriers, who incidentally have no idea of what's going to happen. Anyway, the four of them and myself will walk off the plane, get into the back of the two cars, which by that time will have our own people at the wheel and riding shotgun in the front. We'll simply drive out of the airport and instead of driving to the bank, we'll drive straight across the border into Spain. Freddie and Alex will take care of the four couriers and we'll dump them somewhere en-route. We can be across the border in twenty-five minutes if they put their foot down, then we just board the plane waiting for us at Seville airport and be on our way to Dubai before anyone realises what's happened.'

‘Are you sure the police won’t be escorting or following the two cars?’

‘Yes, I’m sure. We were offered an escort, but I turned it down saying they would just attract attention to us, and that’s the last thing we want.’

‘Are the plane and pilot booked?’

‘Yes Dom, stop worrying. It’s a large Lear jet hired in a bogus company name, and we’re all booked on board. It’s goodbye to Europe forever for all of us.’

‘Right, I’ll go and see her ladyship. Cheers Francois.’

‘Bye Dom.’

We then heard the clicks as the phones cut off and Richard turned the recording off.

‘My God!’ exclaimed Paul. ‘The bastards are actually going for it.’

‘Thanks Kurt,’ said Stephen thoughtfully, ‘but what I really don’t understand is why Viljoen talked so openly on his own mobile. That worries me and it is most unlike him. I don’t understand why he didn’t use a burner phone.’

‘He did,’ said Kurt with a broad grin on his face. ‘Once we’d decided to tap various phones it occurred to me that any information would have to start with Viljoen. As you know we were box-tailing him everywhere he went, and yesterday he called in at a mobile phone shop and bought something, although we couldn’t see what.’

‘Sorry to interrupt, Kurt,’ said Sam, ‘but what on earth is box-tailing?’

‘We literally put a box of tails or as you call them watchers around whoever we’re following, in this case we used four of our people, all well disguised. A white guy in his mid-forties with a Zapata style moustache and wearing clear glasses, neatly dressed in a casual shirt and slacks, a young black guy dressed in tatty jeans, wearing sunglasses and a pair of headphones strapped on his head, an elderly lady who looked to be in her sixties, although she is in fact only thirty three and very fit, and lastly we had a motor cycle cop in bikers leathers on an unmarked motor bike. They form a box around the person they're watching, and whichever direction the object of their attention takes, the nearest person takes over as the prime watcher while the other three reform the box around him. The motor cycle is there in case he suddenly jumps in a car and drives off.'

'Thank you, sorry to have interrupted.'

Kurt continued.

'As soon as the tail came over the radio saying that he'd gone into a mobile phone shop, I instructed one of the team to go into the shop once Viljoen had left, stick his Interpol ID card under the nose of whoever had served him, and get all the details of his purchase. I also instructed the tail that if the shop assistant failed to give us the information we wanted, then he was to be told he was immediately being charged for aiding and abetting a known terrorist, and that he would be taken straight to prison where he would be tried in secret for treason—which carries the death penalty in South Africa. Actually we couldn't do any of that, but he wouldn't know, and threat of the death penalty is usually enough to scare the shit out of anyone and it usually gets us any information we need.'

'And you got the information?' asked Stephen.

'Oh yes. Viljoen had bought himself a "pay-as-you-go" mobile, and the shop assistant gave us the phone's number straight away. We immediately tapped into it and recorded the conversation you've just listened to.'

'Well done, Kurt,' said Paul.

'So,' said Paulo, 'it looks like this gang are planning to take over the two unmarked cars somewhere en-route to Faro airport, murder the four couriers who could obviously identify them all, and then simply drive off with the stones. Do we know which company Viljoen has got the cars and drivers from?'

'No, I'm sorry. That's one bit of information I don't have. Is that something you can find out, Paulo, with a few discreet enquiries?'

'No need, Paulo, I already know,' said Stephen. 'Markus called me and said De Beers have contracts with private car hire companies all over the world, and Viljoen booked the usual Portuguese company. I guess he thought it would have looked suspicious if he'd used someone else.'

'So who is it,' I asked.

'It's a company called "Damazio Serviços Lda," replied Stephen.

'Lda?' queried Helena.

'That's the Portuguese version of our Ltd,' said Paulo.

'So,' I began, 'today's Wednesday and the stones arrive on Friday morning, so I guess we better work out how we're going to protect the stones, save the lives of the couriers if possible, and grab the gang.'

And that's what we spent the rest of the day planning.

Chapter Thirty-Three

Friday morning arrived and we all met bright and early at our hotel in Vilamoura. De Beers's plane with Viljoen, the four couriers and the stones on board was in the air having flown from South Africa to Cameroon where it stopped briefly for refuelling. Interpol had a man in the control tower at Douala International Airport, and he had radioed through to us that the refuelled plane had taken off for Faro.

'Right,' said Stephen, 'I guess we all need to get into position although we've still got three hours before they arrive.'

'Do we have any idea where they're planning to take over the cars?' asked Sam.

'Haven't a clue,' replied Stephen, 'and it bothers me tremendously. The watchers in Spain have told us that Derek Simpson, along with Jimmy Priestley, Alex Donovan and Freddie Drayton have all left Mijas in Derek's Bentley, and Sandra Simpson and Dominic St Clair have left in her BMW, also heading in this direction.'

'Our watchers also said that Derek, Jimmy, Alex and Freddie are all wearing grey suits, white shirts and black ties, i.e., the same outfits Damazio Serviços drivers wear.'

'So it's those four that are going to take over the Mercs,' said Paul, 'and my bet is that Sandra and Dominic are heading straight to Seville airport and the Learjet.'

'I'm not bothered about those two,' said Kurt, 'we have two of our people at Seville airport, both dressed in mechanic's overalls, and they will start work on the engine cowling of the Learjet about fifteen minutes before the other four arrive. Our lads will remove a vital bit of equipment so that the engine won't start and they can't possibly take off, and then we all move in and arrest the lot of them at Seville Airport. We have to let the other four steal the stones and we have to let them all try and flee the country, and that way we have a cast iron case against the lot of them, Viljoen included, when it all goes to court.'

'Do we have anyone watching Damazio Serviços?' asked Sam.

'Yes,' replied Kurt. 'They are based at an industrial estate just outside Faro, and we have a couple of guys temporarily working for the removal company in the adjacent unit. They are keeping an eye on the two cars and will radio in the minute the cars leave.'

'Will they follow them?' I asked.

'No, not as such,' said Kurt. 'Our guys have put tracking bleepers underneath the two Mercs and we will be about five minutes behind them. They will let us know what is happening as much as they can, but they have strict instructions not to interfere. I know this sounds really rough on the Damazio drivers, but we have to let Simpson and his gang take over the cars, steal the diamonds and head to Seville. If we don't, we'll have bugger all to charge them with and they'll just take off to Dubai as soon as they're bailed, and with the UAE not accepting extradition orders we'll never get them back and into court.'

'So what do we do?' asked Sam.

'We wait,' said Kurt. 'We just wait.' And that's just what we did.

Richard, who was manning the radio came into the conference room and said the Mercs were just leaving their depot, with two men in each car.

'OK everyone,' said Stephen, 'I know this feels wrong, but we have to let this pan out and take its course. I suggest we all get in our vehicles and head for Seville airport. Richard has got portable radio gear and, there's a two-way radio receiver in each car. Richard will keep us all informed as to what's happening as soon as he knows.'

We went down to the hotel's car park, and Sam and Helena came with me in my Jag. Richard took the front passenger seat in Stephen's hire car, a silver Range Rover, meanwhile Kurt and Paulo travelled with Paul in his hire car, a silver Ford Mondeo. Most hire cars in Portugal seem to be silver. Strictly speaking, we weren't supposed to take Portuguese hire cars across the border into Spain, but I don't think Hertz were going to be prosecuting Interpol, even if they did find out. Kurt and Stephen had already had two long phone conversations and a lengthy meeting with Comisario General Carlos Bautista, the regional head of the Spanish "Guardia Civil", their version of the police, and he'd been more than happy to co-operate with Interpol. Initially he wasn't very happy about relinquishing jurisdiction to the Metropolitan police, but when Kurt explained that all the criminals were British, and that they hadn't actually committed any crimes in Spain, he reluctantly agreed to let Stephen take them back to the UK for prosecution. But they had to catch them first.

We were driving along the incredibly boring stretch of motorway between the Portuguese / Spanish border and Seville when Richard's voice came over the radio.

'It's started. The Simpsons have taken over the two Merc's. Our two guys from the removals company knew the route and were following the Mercs at a distance. They found the Damazio's men a couple of minutes ago. They said all four of them are unconscious, but alive. They'd all been drugged and not killed thank God, and then dragged behind some bushes. Tom, one of our guys, said they would have missed them, but fortunately they arrived just in time to see the two Mercs driving off, and so they stopped and had a look round. They found all four of them unconscious behind the bushes. Tom also said it looks like they've all been injected with something or other as they found four syringes. Paulo suggested Tom take all four of the Damazio men to Gambelas as quickly as possible, and not to wait for an ambulance. Gambelas is a private hospital near Faro, and Paulo told Tom to take the syringes with them. They've got all the facilities to look after the men there, and also find out what they've been given.'

'Well let's hope they drug the couriers as well, rather than kill them,' said Helena.

We continued driving and eagerly awaited the next update. We didn't have long to wait.

'Our surveillance guys at Faro airport said it went as smooth as silk. The two Mercs pulled up alongside the Learjet, Viljoen got off carrying a large bag, which we assume contains the uncut diamonds, he then climbed into the back of the black Merc being driven by Jimmy Priestly with Derek Simpson in the back, and they drove out of the airport. Freddie and Alex followed in the silver Merc. Alex is driving, by the way.'

'What happened to the couriers?' I asked.

'Thankfully they'd all been drugged on the plane rather than killed,' said Kurt over the radio, 'and we found them all unconscious once we boarded the plane.' Richard, can you please radio the guys at Faro airport and tell them to arrest the four couriers when they eventually regain consciousness. We'll sort out the paperwork of who is and who isn't guilty later. Just don't let anyone get away, and for God's sake don't let that plane take off.'

Stephen came on the radio.

'We must assume, boys and girls, that Derek Simpson and co. are now following us all on the road to Seville airport. Can I suggest that we speed it up and ensure we're all in position long before they arrive?'

'One thing Stephen?' I said over the radio. 'They may come quietly when we arrive, but I doubt it, and knowing Freddie as we do, I don't think he'll take it lying down. If he's armed, which I'm sure he will be, he's liable to start shooting, and none of us are armed.'

'Don't worry Michael, we won't be doing the arresting. The idea is to let them all get to the plane, and then Comisario General Bautista and thirty of his men in armed jeeps will drive out and surround their plane. Every one of those thirty officers will be armed to the teeth with automatic machine guns, and even Freddie Drayton isn't daft enough to take on those odds. Once they're all disarmed and in handcuffs, we'll arrive, read them their rights and take them into custody.'

We arrived at the airport, and Comisario General Carlos Bautista was there to meet us.

'Ah, Senor Meisner, so nice to meet you at last. Inspector Stephen here has told me all about you during our long talks.

'Just Kurt please,' he replied.

They shook hands and then Stephen handled the introductions. Kurt then briefed everyone.

'As you know Comisario, we have two Interpol operatives posing as flight engineers, and I am informed that they have already been out to the aircraft and removed an important component which will ensure the plane will never take off. The pilot is innocent in all of this, but he has not been informed of what is going on. He will obviously just plead ignorance as to why the plane will not start. Once both of the Mercs have arrived and the passengers have all got out, can your men please drive out and surround the plane?'

'Yes, we can do this. Tell me Mr Kurt, is anyone liable to start shooting at my officers? If so, I cannot guarantee anyone's safety. My men will react automatically and will return fire. Thirty automatic machine guns will cause many deaths I am afraid.'

'I think it's highly unlikely anyone will start shooting,' replied Kurt particularly when they see that they are up against thirty officers, all armed with automatic weapons, and all wearing bullet proof vests.'

'In that case I see you will have no problems,' said the Comisario. 'Let us all take our best positions and wait the arrival of your criminals.'

I loved the way the Comisario spoke his English, very polite, but not quite right!

It took about twenty-five minutes for the two Mercs to arrive at Seville airport. The black one driven by Jimmy drove to the foot of the aircraft's staircase, and Alex's silver Merc pulled in right behind it. It was a really strange situation. We could see quite clearly what was happening, but we couldn't hear a single word being spoken. The men all got out of the cars, meanwhile Sandra and Dominic came down the aircraft's steps to greet them. Derek and Sandra high fived each other, then hugged and kissed, while the rest of them shook hands and patted each other's backs. They were all obviously overjoyed that they just got away with stealing three hundred and seventy five million pounds worth of uncut diamonds.

Suddenly eight jeeps came roaring into view, with their sirens screaming a deafening noise, blue and red lights flashing like mad and each jeep containing four officers pointing machine guns at the Simpsons and their entourage. The gang all looked at each other and then slowly raised their hands in surrender, all that is except Freddie and Alex who decided to make a run for it. One of the Guardia officers fired a burst of his machine gun over their heads and they both stopped in their tracks. Comisario Bautista arrived in another police jeep and he had them all searched thoroughly. He found automatic pistols on Freddie, Alex and Jimmy. Freddie also had an automatic pistol tucked in his right sock, plus two very sharp knives in a belt round his waist. Having disarmed them, they were all thrown roughly to the ground, including Sandra Simpson, then they were all handcuffed from behind and told to stand. It was at this point that we all arrived in two more Spanish jeeps.

'Well, well,' began Stephen as he got out of the car, 'the elusive Mr Derek Simpson and the delectable Sandra, although I don't suppose either of you remember me?'

'I can't remember your name,' said Sandra Simpson through gritted teeth, 'but I thought I could smell you coming a mile off. All you filth have that distinctive stink.'

'Say nothing,' said Dominic. 'We're on Spanish soil and we've committed no crime in Spain. Keep quiet and there's nothing they can do. They'll have to release us all.'

'Ah, well, that would be true if the good Comisario here had not agreed to allow the Metropolitan Police to have jurisdiction in all matters as you're all British citizens.'

'You can't do that,' squawked Dominic. 'That's not legal.'

'Oh for God's sake, put a sock in it St Clair,' said Paul, after which he read them all their rights under British law. 'You will all be flown to England where you will be charged with numerous crimes including today's armed robbery, the murder of Malcolm Tisbury along with the theft of his uncut diamonds, plus numerous other crimes around the world including money laundering via the Bahamas.'

'I'm not being done for no murder,' cried Jimmy Priestly, 'the murders were all Freddie's handiwork.'

'You're next on me list, you double crossing bastard,' said an angry Freddie Drayton.

'There is an RAF transport plane waiting by the hanger,' said Stephen, 'and it will give us great pleasure to escort you all back to London where you will be held in custody without bail until your first appearance in court.'

An RAF Lockheed C-130J Hercules had touched down on the runway at Seville airport two and a half hours earlier, and it had come with a compliment of twelve well-armed Royal Marines. Sandra and Derek Simpson, Freddie Drayton, Jimmy Priestly, Alex Donovan, Dominic St Clair and Francois Viljoen were all taken on board and handcuffed to a steel rail behind them which ran the full length of the plane's fuselage. Stephen and Paul also flew to England with them on the Hercules, while Sam, Paulo, Richard, Kurt, Helena and I all drove back to the Algarve with Kurt driving Stephen's hired Range Rover and Paulo driving Paul's Mondeo. Having returned the hire cars, the six of us had a very sociable meal together at a local Chinese restaurant, after which Paulo went home, and Kurt and Helena returned to the hotel to book flights to their respective homes. Richard cleared and boxed up all his equipment, and then arranged flights to London for all the gear and himself. As for us—Sam and I went back to the villa and had a very early night.

To be honest, I thought the case of the Mijas Murderer, as I was now calling it, was all done and dusted, but then a couple of weeks after we'd returned, Stephen telephoned me to say Sam and I would be required to give evidence at their trial in London.

'Because there are several murders involved as well as the thefts, the case will be tried at the Old Bailey. I'm really sorry Michael, I was originally hoping to leave you and Sam out of this, but I'm afraid your evidence will now be vital in so many areas where the rest of us just weren't present, and therefore can't testify.'

The Old Bailey is in fact the slang name for the Central Criminal Court of England and Wales, and it dates back to the sixteenth century, with the present building standing on the site of the medieval Newgate Gaol. I suddenly realised Stephen was talking again.

'Interpol have now arrested several others including Pieter Van Straaten and Jan Joubert in Cape Town, who as far as we can tell at this stage are the only two couriers involved apart from Viljoen. They've also been to the Bahamas where they found both Jeremy Green and Caroline Chambers who thought they'd be safe there. They also arrested Naomi

Gardiner and Casandra Dufreine in the Bahamas and finally Hannes de Jaeger in Amsterdam.'

'Good grief Stephen, they're going to need a hell of a big dock at the Old Bailey. I make that fourteen of them in all. When's the trial scheduled for?'

'Oh don't panic, it's month's away yet, probably February or March next year. I'll let you know as soon as we've got the date. Bye for now Michael and love to Sam.'

Chapter Thirty-Four

The trial date was set for the middle of March, and in the intervening period, Sam and I had officially got engaged when I asked her to marry me during an excellent meal at our favourite restaurant. Thankfully she said yes, even though I was incredibly boring and refused to go down on one knee in the middle of a restaurant. We had a great engagement party a month later, and in addition to our regular friends who lived around us in the Algarve, we also invited everyone who had worked with us on the case. Yes, they were all work colleagues, but without doubt, they had all become really good friends. Kurt even made it back to the Algarve having taken some well-earned and greatly overdue holiday.

The trial when it came lasted just over eleven weeks, with Sam and myself in the witness box for several weeks. Also in the box for the prosecution at various times were Kurt, Helena, Stephen, Paul, Richard and Markus who insisted on giving evidence. The defence comprised of the defendants all giving each other false alibis which the judge and the jury saw through immediately. Thankfully the jury in the case were all very wise people and they returned guilty verdicts on everyone involved in less than an hour. The judge stated several times during his summing up of the case that he had been horrified at the degree of viciousness involved, and the lack of respect to human life shown by every one of the defendants, and his sentencing showed it.

Sandra and Derek Simpson were sentenced first, and they both received twenty-five years in prison as the instigators and ring leaders, with Derek as we later discovered being sent straight to Wakefield prison from the court. At their age it's extremely unlikely they will ever get out of prison, or for that matter ever see each other again. Francois Viljoen, Jimmy Priestly and Alex Donovan all received sentences of twelve years and were all sent to Wandsworth Prison. Dominic St Clair hadn't been involved in any of the violence, but he had grossly abused his position as a lawyer to help in the commitment of the crimes, and as such he also got twelve years and was sent to Belmarsh prison, as well as being struck off for life from acting as a licensed lawyer in both the UK and Spain. I suppose when he eventually does get out he could go and ply his trade in South America, where I'm sure he could find himself lots of business with Columbia's drug barons.

As for Freddie Drayton, I am delighted to say he was eventually convicted on seven different counts of murder, and was sentenced to life imprisonment in Broadmoor with no leave to appeal, and no chance of ever being granted parole. The judge said it was his sick mind resulting in his method of cutting innocent victims throats that ensured he could not be incarcerated with other prisoners in a normal jail, and it also meant he will never be released. Both Jan Joubert and Pieter Van Straaten were sentenced to three years each, and they were shipped back to South Africa to do their time in Drakenstein Correctional Centre.

Drakenstein was formally known as Victor Verster Prison, and was made famous for being the location